# THERE WERE FOUR OF THEM

Two boys, David and Peter.
Two girls, Sandy and Rhoda.

Each was very different. But on the lush island resort, all were drawn together by the same needs, the same desperation, into a private world.

They were kids who had everything—but they wanted more. And what they wanted was horrifying beyond belief.

"A fine piece of writing that rings true all the way"—Cleveland Press

"You'll find LAST SUMMER very hard to forget"—Cosmopolitan

# LAST
## SUMMER

Evan Hunter

A SIGNET BOOK from
NEW AMERICAN LIBRARY
TIMES MIRROR

SIGNET TRADEMARK REG. U.S. PAT. OFF. AND FOREIGN COUNTRIES
REGISTERED TRADEMARK—MARCA REGISTRADA
HECHO EN CHICAGO, U.S.A.

SIGNET, SIGNET CLASSICS, SIGNETTE, MENTOR AND PLUME BOOKS
*are published by The New American Library, Inc.,
1301 Avenue of the Americas, New York, New York 10019*

FIRST PRINTING, APRIL, 1969

PRINTED IN THE UNITED STATES OF AMERICA

*This is for my mother and father,*
*Marie and Charles Lombino*

*Sudden in a shaft of sunlight*
*Even while the dust moves*
*There rises the hidden laughter*
*Of children in the foliage.*

T. S. ELIOT

# ONE:

~~~~~~~~~~~~~~

## *THE GULL*

WE SPENT LAST SUMMER, WHEN I WAS JUST SIXTEEN, on an island mistakenly named Greensward, its shores only thinly vegetated with beach grass and plum, its single forest destroyed by fire more than twenty years before. There were perhaps fifty summer homes on the island, most of them gray and clustered safely on the bay side, the remainder strung out along the island's flanks and on the point jutting insanely into the Atlantic.

It was there that the sea was wildest. It was there that we first met Sandy.

She was standing close to the shoreline as David and I came up the beach behind her, spume exploding on her left, pebbles rolling and tossing in a muddy backwash, a tall girl wearing a white bikini, her hair the color of the dunes, a pale gold that fell loose and long about her face. Her head was studiously bent. Hands on hips, legs widespread, she stood tense and silent, studying something in the sand at her feet. It was a very hot day. The sky over the ocean seemed stretched too tight. An invisible sun seared the naked beach, turning everything intensely white, the bursting waves dissolving into foam, the glaring sky, the endless stretch of sand, the girl standing motionless, her pale hair only faintly stirring. We approached on her left, walking between her and the ocean, turning for a look at her face, her small breasts in the scanty bra top, the gentle curve of her hips above the white bikini pants, the long line of her legs.

The thing lying at her feet in the sand was a sea gull.

"He's still alive," she said suddenly, and raised her head to meet our gaze.

Her eyes were a vivid blue, set wide, her nose narrow, flaring suddenly at the nostrils, combining with a full upper lip that curled outward and away from her teeth to give her face a feral look. I guessed she was about fifteen years old. We looked down at the gull. He was a large bird, gray and white. His eyes were closed. He kept working his beak, as though trying to suck in air.

"Yes, he's alive," David said.

We were standing with the sun behind us. David was taller than I last summer, a strapping six-footer who'd been lifting weights for four years, ever since he was twelve. I'd always liked his looks, from the first day I met him. He had broad shoulders even then, a narrow waist, chest and abdominal muscles as clean as Alley Oop's. His eyes were blue, flecked with white, his hair a dusty blond. He had good features, too, and a strong jaw and brow; he looked solid and reliable. My own appearance last summer suggested a sort of vague maturity. I was trying very hard to achieve a sophisticated look, so I wore my brown hair long and combed sideways across my forehead, almost hiding my eyes, which were also brown. But my nose was growing faster than the rest of my face, and my mouth was sprinkled with acne at one corner, and it was pretty difficult to maintain a cool against such odds.

"Get out of the sun," the girl said, "he needs the sun."

"The bird?"

"Can't you see he's dying?"

"What's that got to do with the sun?"

"What happened to him, anyway?" David asked.

"I don't know. I was just walking along, and there he was."

"Which house are you in?" I asked.

"Up the beach. The Stern house."

"What's your name?" David said.

"Sandy."

"I'm David. This is Peter."

"Hi," I said.

"Hi. Will you help me take him off the beach?"

"What for?"

"Get him out of the sun," Sandy said.

David and I looked at each other.

"Gulls are pretty dirty animals," David said.

"He'll die if we don't help him," Sandy said.

"He'll die anyway," I said.

"Never mind, I'll do it myself," Sandy said.

She brushed a strand of hair away from her face, getting sand on her cheek, and then walked off toward the dune while David and I watched. She almost fell climbing the dune, but neither of us dared laugh. She disappeared into the tall beach grass and came back with a large weathered shingle which she carried directly to where the bird was lying on his back in the sand. She did not look at us. Her face was very serious as she bent over the bird and started to shove the shingle under him. The bird gave a shriek just then, and tried to flap his wings. Sandy dropped the shingle, and screamed. She started to turn, and then in her haste merely backpedaled away from the noisy bird, her eyes wide, her mouth still open around the scream.

"You rats," she said, standing at a respectable distance from the bird, who was now silent, "why won't you help me?"

"Because we don't want to get bit," I said.

"You can get rabies from those damn things," David said.

"Oh, rabies, my ass," Sandy said, and walked back to the gull again, frowning. Gingerly, she picked up the shingle and then cautiously edged it under the bird, who remained motionless and silent this time. Holding him out at arm's length on the shingle, she began walking toward the dune again. We followed her. The bird at-

tempted to flap his wings again, but all he could manage
was a weak flutter. All the while, he kept sucking in air,
his beak working. When my grandmother was dying of
cancer at New York Hospital, she looked the same
way. My father said to me in the corridor outside,
"Your grandmother is dying," and I said, "I know," but
all could think of was how disgusting she looked
trying to suck in air through her open mouth.

Sandy walked up over the dune and then onto the
boardwalk, a narrow path about two feet wide, made
up of wooden slats loosely strung together. David and I
kept following her at a distance, perhaps ten feet or so
behind her. When she reached her house, she climbed
up onto the deck, put the gull on his shingle down in
the shade, walked to the screen door, turned to us before she opened it, and said, "Watch him. I'll be right
back."

The screen door banged shut behind her. We turned
to watch the bird. Nothing happened. That is, nothing
different. He didn't shriek again, or try to flap his
wings, but neither did he die. He simply lay there on his
shingle, moving his beak spasmodically, trying to suck
in air. The surf was extremely rough that day. The
Stern house, which Sandy was living in that summer,
was up on a dune perhaps a hundred yards from the
shore. I could hear the waves pounding in, and then
echoing on the air, a strange vast hollow sound, like
voices in an angry argument very far away.

"He'll die," David said.

"Mm." I was thinking of my grandmother. I had
never liked her, anyway.

"I wonder what happened to him."

"Maybe he flew into something."

"What could he have flown into?"

"Another bird?"

"Maybe," David said.

We kept looking down at the gull.

"What do you suppose she's doing in there?"

"I don't know."

"Maybe we ought to split."

"No, let's see if he dies," David said.

Sandy came out about five minutes later with an old towel and a bowl of hot soup. She bent over the gull and wrapped him in the towel, holding the poor bird's wings against his body while she did so. Then she took out a spoon she had tucked into the bra part of her bikini, dipped some soup out of the bowl, and carefully brought it to the gull's beak.

"You've got to be kidding," David said.

"Shut up," Sandy said.

"She thinks she's in a Walt Disney movie."

"Shut up."

"You're only going to kill him quicker," David said.

"He's in shock," Sandy answered, and tilted the soup into his open beak. Naturally, the bird gave another shriek. She backed away from him again, but she wasn't quite as frightened this time, maybe because he was all wrapped up in the towel and couldn't move.

"See?" she said, as if she had proved some idiotic point.

"Yeah, he doesn't like it," David said.

"Gulls like everything," Sandy said. "They eat all kinds of crap," and glanced toward the screen door. I figured her mother was inside the house. "See?" she said, forcing more soup down his throat. "He *does* like it."

"He's going to have convulsions any minute," I said.

"No, he won't."

"Besides, gulls are scavengers. You should let him die."

"Sure," David said. "They're like sharks."

"He's a sweet old bird," Sandy said, and fed him another spoonful of soup.

"Wait'll that sweet old bird bites you," David said.

"What kind of soup *is* that?" I asked.

"Chicken noodle."

"It smells good."

"You can have what's left over."

"Thanks, from *his* mouth?"

"What're you gonna do with that damn bird, anyway?" David asked.

"Make him my pet."

"What'll he do, sleep at the foot of your bed?"

"What'll you name him? Rover?"

Sandy didn't even look up at us. She merely kept spooning soup into the bird's mouth. I was sure he would choke at any moment. Finally, she put down the spoon and the bowl, and stood up, and nodded, and walked toward the screen door again. "Watch him," she said, and again she went inside. We looked at the bird. He didn't look any better than he had on the beach.

"I give him about ten minutes," David said.

"Five."

"Maybe less."

"That soup sure smells good."

"Why don't you finish it?" David said, and gave me an elbow and a grin.

"Yeah, yeah." I looked at the gull again. "You think its a male?"

"I don't know."

"How can you tell if it is or not?"

"The males have pricks, same as you and me."

"Shh," I said, and glanced toward the screen door.

David shrugged. "When he dies," he said, "we'll take a look."

"*If* he does."

"Oh, he'll die, all right."

"Not if *she* has anything to say about it."

"A sea gull for a pet," David said, and shook his head.

"I knew a girl at camp had a raccoon for a pet."

"Raccoons aren't sea gulls." He boosted himself up onto the deck railing. The sun was behind him, limning his head. He began humming. The bird gave a little peep just then, as though trying to sing along.

"When he dies," I said, "let's go over to The Captain's for some hamburgers."

"Okay," David said.

"You want to ask *her* to come?"

"She'll probably have to attend the funeral," David said.

The screen door swung open.

"Is he still alive?" Sandy asked.

"I figure another three or four minutes," David said, and winked at me.

"Go to hell," Sandy said. This time she did not bother to look toward the screen door. She was holding a long piece of clothesline in her hand.

"What're you gonna do with that?" I asked.

"You'll see," she said, and bent down over the bird again. His feet were sticking out of the bottom of the towel, he looked like a consumptive old man at a Turkish bath. Sandy knotted one end of the clothesline around his right leg, and then carried the other end to the deck railing. She looped it swiftly around one of the stanchions, made a double knot in it, stood up, put her hands on her hips and said, "There."

"Very good," David said. "You've got a half-dead bird tied to the deck railing."

"All I need now is a box," she said, and went into the house again.

"I think she's nuts," David said.

"I do, too. Let's split."

"Look at him."

We both looked. He was still working his beak, gasping for air, his eyes closed.

"What's that in his neck there?" David said.

"Where?"

"There, what is that thing?"

"Where? I don't see . . ."

"Look at it! Can't you see it?"

"Oh, God!"

"That's a fishhook. He's swallowed a fishhook!"

"Oh, man, that's disgusting."

"Sure, that's the tip sticking out of his neck!"

"God, *look* at that!"

"What is it?" Sandy said, rushing out of the house. The screen door slammed shut behind her. The deck was suddenly very still.

"He's got a fishhook caught in his throat," David said.

Sandy looked down at the gull. She was carrying a cardboard box which she dropped to the deck behind her. Then she knelt quietly beside the bird and stared at the protruding tip of the hook.

"I didn't see it," she said, "did you? I mean *before*?"

"No," David said.

"I didn't see it, either."

"But there's no blood."

"No."

"You'll have to take it out," Sandy said.

"Me?" David said. "You're out of your mind."

"Please," she said.

"Absolutely not."

"I couldn't do it, really," she said. "I can't even take one out of a fish."

"Uh-uh, not me," David said.

"Peter?" she said, and looked up. I didn't answer at first. She kept looking at me, her eyes on my face, one hand extended toward me. "He'll die otherwise."

"So what?" David said. "He's just a crumby gull."

She did not take her eyes from me. Her voice had sounded doubtful, but her eyes were confident; she knew damn well I couldn't leave that hook in the bird's throat.

"All right," I said, "hold him."

"Who?" David said.

"Come on."

*"Me?"*

"I'll hold him," Sandy said.

"Never mind, I'll hold him," David said. "I swear to God, if he bites me . . ."

"He won't bite you."

"Okay, let's do it already," I said.

"I'll hold his feet," Sandy said.

"We don't need anybody to hold his feet," David said. "Just get the hell out of the way." He made a move toward the bird's head, and just then the beak opened and closed again. He pulled his hand back, watching the bird warily. Then he reached out suddenly with both hands and grabbed the beak, immediately forcing it open. "Hurry up," he said, "pull the damn thing out."

I got the hook out pretty fast, considering. There wasn't any blood while it was still in the gull's throat, but the minute I eased it loose, the blood began to flow, pouring into the bird's ruff. David got some on his hands; I could just imagine how much *that* thrilled him. I kept thinking of my grandmother. I was wondering why someone hadn't stuck his hand down her open throat and pulled out the cancer, just the way I'd pulled out the hook. Sandy ran inside for peroxide and bandages, and finally we got the gull all cleaned up and bandaged and tucked away in his towel inside the cardboard box, with one leg tied to the porch railing.

So we asked Sandy, after all, if she'd like to have a hamburger with us down at The Captain's.

That Saturday night, they held a dance at the firehouse for all the teenage kids on the island.

The firehouse was down by the bay, the first thing you saw when you came over from the mainland. It was almost directly back of the ferry slip, and on the right of it was the post office, and on the left was the general store run by Mr. Porter, who everyone said was a millionaire, but which probably wasn't true. The firehouse was built in 1945 immediately after the big fire that destroyed the pine forest in the center of the island. The forest had always terrified me. I had been to it only once or twice, but it was the bleakest spot imaginable, with charred dead Australian pines, a ghostlike silence hanging over the entire place. Just miles and miles of burned-out trees, black and twisted against the sky, surrounded by stunted second growth.

The dance at the firehouse had about forty chaperones to supervise three-dozen kids. A table was set up just inside the door, with Mr. Gorham sitting behind it taking admissions, and with a little cash box near his right hand. We gave him fifty cents apiece (actually, David gave him a buck for both of us, knowing I'd square it with him later), and then we went in and stood close to the table; it's always difficult coming into a dance, even if you know all the kids there. A tall pretty girl was standing across the room, near the ladders hanging on the cinder-block wall. She didn't even look at us. She had red hair cut in bangs across her forehead and coming down to about the nape of her neck.

"Who's that?" I said.

"Where?"

"There. Near the ladders."

"The redhead?"

"Yeah."

"I don't know."

We looked at her again, and she looked back at us this time and then let her gaze wander right past us. The expression on her face was very sophisticated and cool, as though she had only inadvertently stumbled into these teenage proceedings and was utterly bored to tears.

"Let's find out who she is," I said.

"Okay," David said, and shrugged, and we started across the room toward her. She was still being very blasé, her eyes smokily and lazily taking in the surroundings, her beautiful red hair clipped sharp and clean like a copper helmet—oh my, she just couldn't

have cared less for all these grubby little children mill-
ing around. And then, when we were about three feet
away from her, she suddenly turned toward us, her blue
eyes snapping, her mouth twisting up into a triumphant
little grin. She bent over almost double, the way a fast-
draw gunslick does in a Western movie, slapped her
thigh with one hand, drew an imaginary pistol,
straight-armed it at us, and shouted, "Ha, *got* you!"

It was Sandy.

She looked great. In addition to the red wig, she was
wearing a blue sweater and chinos, and she was barefoot, with a gold bracelet on her left ankle. We walked
around her, appraising the wig. She did a little model's
turn for us, with her head and nose tilted up, and then
said, "What do you think?"

"Where'd you get it?"

"It's my mother's."

"It's wild."

"It cost three hundred and fifty dollars."

"Where's your own hair?" I asked.

"I've got it up with pins."

"Under the wig?"

"Where do you think, under my arm?"

"It's terrific," I said.

"How old do I look?" Sandy said.

"Seventy-two," David said.

"Come on."

"She wants you to say nineteen."

"Nineteen," David said.

"Do I really?"

"You look like a fifteen-year-old girl wearing a red
wig," David said.

"Is that a wig?" a boy standing next to me asked.

"No, it's a locomotive," I answered.

"Ha-ha," the boy said.

I didn't know who he was, but it became immediately
plain that he had an excellent sense of humor because

the next thing he said was, "Are you bald or something?" which Sandy didn't even bother to answer.

Something was beginning to happen.

I couldn't quite understand it. But I felt it came over me all at once, and I sensed that David and Sandy were suddenly aware of it as well. It had something to do with the wig, I knew, the fact that the wig was a disguise. It had something to do with how beautiful the wig made Sandy look, older, and sophisticated, and experienced, somewhat like a college senior. But I suddenly felt that I myself, and David too, looked extremely handsome in the identical light-blue tee shirts we had bought at Mr. Porter's, so that there was a unity to the trio we formed—Sandy in the center with her red wig and dark-blue sweater, David and I flanking her in light blue—a harmony. This sudden unity, this certain knowledge that each of us was aware of his own good looks as well as the effect we created together, led to an intense feeling of pride, again shared. For a moment I found it difficult to disassociate myself from Sandy and David, to look upon myself as a single entity.

The three of us together had performed a delicate piece of bird surgery two days ago, and now a sense of secret intimacy flashed between us like electricity, hot and bright and feeding on itself, generating new power from its own violent discharge. Every kid in that firehouse was looking at us, I felt, and being dazzled by us, and wishing he could be a part of us. I could actually see kids trying to get *near* us, as though wanting to be absorbed, longing to be touched by our special glow. We were three very bright and searing, no—*one* enormously powerful life-giving sun that had suddenly erupted into the universe, diminishing by its brilliance all previously existing stars.

I'm a very bad dancer, but I asked Sandy to dance anyway, and it didn't bother me at all that I wasn't as good as some of the other kids on the floor. We got into a conversation about the gull, and we were so very involved in it, so *totally* involved in the blinding glare that was only ourselves, that there just didn't seem to be anyone else in the room. She started telling me about the leash and collar she had bought at Mr. Porter's, both in a bright red which she thought would go nicely with the bird's gray and white feathers. She hadn't put the collar on him as yet, she explained, because the hole in his neck still hadn't healed. She had to time this very carefully because she didn't want to interfere with the healing, but neither did she want him roaming around loose or flying off when he got stronger.

"Do you think I should clip his wings?" she asked.

"Not unless you want to break that poor bird's spirit," I said.

"Peter, please be serious."

"No, I don't think you should clip his wings."

"I don't think so, either."

"The leash and collar will take care of the situation fine."

"Yes, I think so. I've still got him tied to the porch railing," she said. "He won't fly away, that's for sure, but he's beginning to get pretty active."

"You'd better get that leash on him."

"I will. Do you think I'll be able to train him?"

"Yes, gulls are very intelligent."

"Oh, good."

"Or crows, I forget which one."

"You're a great help."

"Are you patient?"

"I'm very patient."

"Training takes a lot of patience."

"I told you I'm very patient."

"How do you like the way I dance?"

"You're terrible."

"Yes, thank you."

"But I love you, anyway," she said, and that was when the fellow who had asked her if she was bald cut in. He did it in a very gentlemanly manner, I thought.

I immediately released Sandy, gave a short little bow, and began moving away. But, glancing back, I saw Sandy pull a face over his shoulder, so I walked over to David and told him to cut right back in.

I went outside while they were dancing, over to the Coke machine in front of Mr. Porter's. I was standing there drinking when the fellow who'd made the "bald" joke walked over. He was wearing sawed-off dungarees, blue sneakers, and a Charlie Brown sweatshirt. He had black hair, which he wore in a very short crew cut, thick black brows, a beefy face. I couldn't see the color of his eyes because he was standing with the light from the firehouse behind him. He was big, about seventeen years old, I guessed, though not as big as David.

"What are you, *wise* guys?" he said.

Usually, when somebody makes a brilliant remark like that one, I'll walk away immediately because it doesn't pay to get into arguments with morons. But that night I didn't feel like walking away, I felt like answering him. Even though he was bigger than me.

So I said, simply, "Yes, we're wise guys."

"Cutting in like that."

"Yes," I said, "cutting in like that."

I tilted the bottle of Coke and drank a little of it, and then I looked at him, and we just stood there outside the store, staring at each other. Or at least *trying* to stare, since it was pretty difficult to locate each other's eyes in the dark. I didn't know what he had in mind, really I didn't. Perhaps a fight, and perhaps not. I've learned, though, that most guys who come over and sound off do so without any intention of starting a fight unless you push them into one, unless you make it absolutely impossible for them to back away. The truth about *this* particular situation was that I felt indestructible. This fellow was at least six feet tall, and very burly in his Charlie Brown sweatshirt, but I wasn't at all afraid of him. In fact, I felt I could knock him flat with a single punch if I had to, walk all over him, squash him into the pier. I felt absolutely courageous and bold and powerful and great. I felt like Batman.

So we kept staring at each other.

"What's your name?" he said.

"Batman," I answered.

"You *are* a wise guy, aren't you?"

"I am a *very* wise guy," I said. "My friend is even wiser. We are the two wisest guys on this whole island, you want to get out of my way?"

He kept staring at me.

"Huh?" I said.

And then he backed off.

Everything exploded inside me, I felt suddenly weak. This was affirmation, you see, concrete affirmation of the fact that I was surrounded by a glow that nothing could penetrate, a magical glow that had somehow been generated by Sandy and David and me, impervious to anyone or anything. With a little fillip, I put the Coke bottle into the crate beside the machine, gave Mr. Charlie Brown Sweatshirt a brief nod, and walked up the pier and into the firehouse without looking back.

"Hey, we were trying to find you," Sandy said. "We want to go crabbing."

"In your wig?" I said.

"No, there aren't any crabs in her wig," David said.

We borrowed a net from the lobster joint on the pier, and then asked Mr. Gorham to lend us his flashlight, which he did reluctantly. It was a marvelous night, with a silver crescent moon in a sky overwhelmed by millions of stars. A mild breeze blew in off the mainland. We could hear the music from the firehouse, the sound of water gently lapping the rotted timbers of the old pier. Sandy flashed the light out over the water in wide probing arcs. The crabs we were after were blue crabs. Whenever we spotted one,

Sandy would lead it in toward the dock, and either David or I would scoop it up into the net. When we caught the first one, we realized we didn't have anything to put it in, so we had to throw it back. I ran up to the firehouse and borrowed one of the red buckets from the wall, dumping the sand out. My friend was still at the dance. When he saw me come in, he moved over to the other side of the room.

We caught six crabs before the dance ended, and then returned the net to the lobster joint and the flashlight to Mr. Gorham. We could have taken a jitney up the beach if we'd wanted to, but we walked all the way home instead, singing. Sandy cooked the crabs the next day, which was Sunday. They were delicious.

On Monday we drank the truth serum.

The truth serum was beer.

"This isn't beer," Sandy said, "it's truth serum."

We were sitting inside the tent we'd constructed by hanging David's poncho from the beach umbrella. Through the open flap facing the ocean, we could see the slanting rain and the gray sea and sky beyond. Each time a wave crashed in against the shore, it left behind it a roiling wake of pebbles and sand, twisted seaweed, splintered rotten wood. The beach looked dirty.

We had walked all the way out to the point in the rain, wearing only our swimsuits; our towels and other stuff were wrapped inside David's poncho. It wasn't until we were putting up the umbrella and fastening the poncho to it that we began to feel a bit chilled. The moment we got inside the tent, we dried ourselves and put on sweaters. Then we spread the blanket and opened the beer. That was when Sandy said it was truth serum.

"It looks like beer to me," David said. "What does it look like to you, Poo?"

"Beer," I said.

"It's truth serum," Sandy insisted. She tilted the bottle to her mouth, drank a little, and then lowered it into her lap. She was sitting with her long legs crossed Indian fashion, a gray sweatshirt covering the top and pants of her bikini. She rolled back her eyes and then intoned, "My middle name is Bernice."

David laughed and said, "I wouldn't tell my middle name if you tortured me."

"Peter?" she said.

I drank a little beer and then, imitating her monotone, said, "My middle name is Albert," and looked surprised, and said, "I think it *is* truth serum, David."

"Try it," Sandy said.

David studied us both solemnly for a moment.

"Go on, David," I said gently. "Try it."

David gave a slight shrug. It seemed to me that he was more interested in *drinking* the beer than in playing games with it. But I knew he wouldn't spoil the fun, and I wasn't surprised when he lifted the bottle to his mouth, drank, put it down, and very quickly and softly said, "My middle name is Lloyd."

"Oh, no!" I said.

"Oh, *yes*," Sandy said. "That's a *wonderful* middle name, what's wrong with it?"

"It's beautiful," I said, "here's to David Lloyd," and I raised my bottle and drank.

"Now you have to tell us another truth," Sandy said.

"Why?"

"Because you just drank some more serum."

"Oh, I see, I see."

"It has to be about yourself," Sandy said.

"Of course."

"So?"

"I flunked geometry when I was a soph," I said.

"Everybody knows that," David said.

"Sandra Bernice didn't know it."

"That's true, I didn't," Sandy said.

"Still and all," David insisted, "if a person is under

the influence of truth serum, he doesn't tell you something stupid like he flunked geometry when he was a soph."

"It *is* stupid to flunk geometry," I said, trying to rescue it.

"But David is right," Sandy said.

"All right," I said. I deliberately took another swallow of beer and then said, "I hate my Uncle Ralph."

"We don't even *know* your Uncle Ralph," David said.

"What difference does that make? I hate him, and that's the truth, and how come I'm the only one drinking?"

"Okay, okay," David said, and drank some beer.

"The truth," Sandy said.

"The truth is this is a pretty idiotic game," David said, and then frowned, thinking. Sandy and I both waited.

"So?" she said at last.

"So okay, wait a minute."

Sandy drank and said, "Major truth: My top is wet."

I drank and said, "Major truth: I like girls who say things like My top is wet."

"I only said it under the influence of the serum," Sandy said.

"I appreciate your honesty."

"Thank you," she said, and nodded.

"You're welcome," I said, and nodded back.

"But the truth is, it *is* wet, and also uncomfortable."

"So take it off," David said, and shrugged.

"Ho-ho," Sandy said, and rolled her eyes.

"Since we are dispensing with crap," I said, and quickly drank, "let me say in all truth . . ."

"No, wait a minute," David said, and drank. He lowered the bottle. "Are you ready?"

"We're ready," I said.

"This is a major truth."

"It better be," Sandy said.

"I hate it when my father swears."

"Does he?"

"All the time."

"What does he say?"

"Everything."

"So what?"

"Well, I think it's undignified for an architect to swear all the time."

"Okay," Sandy said, "that's a major truth."

"Actually," I said, "it's undignified for *anyone* to swear all the time."

"Especially your own father," David said.

Sandy lifted her bottle and drank. "Here's another major truth, are you ready?" She paused, and grinned, and then said, "I love you both."

I drank rapidly and said, "I love you, too."

"Me, too," David said. "Let's drink to it."

We all drank.

"Now we each owe another truth," Sandy said.

"I like this truth serum," I said. "It tastes just like beer."

"We're waiting," Sandy said.

"Why do I always have to go first?"

"You don't," Sandy said. "Here's a truth for you. Mr. Matthews once got funny with me."

"What do you mean?" I said, thinking I knew what she meant, but really shocked to hear it because Mr. Matthews was an island alderman or something and practically in his forties.

"He put his hand under my skirt," Sandy said.

"When?" David asked.

"Last summer."

"What did you do?"

"What *could* I do?"

"You could have screamed or something."

"We were in our living room."

"In your own *house?*"

"Sure, my mother was out in the kitchen."

"And he just stuck his hand under your skirt?"

"Well, he sneaked it under."

"What did he say?"

"He said, 'You're a nice little girl, Sandra,' or some such crap."

"I can't believe it," I said.

"It's true."

"My God, how'll I ever look him in the eye again?"

"Why not?" Sandy said. "It wasn't *your* skirt he had his hand under."

"But he seems like such a nice guy."

"He's a dirty old man," Sandy said, and giggled.

"Isn't he an alderman?"

"He's a councilman."

"An alderman, I thought."

"Whatever he is, he's a swinger," David said, and drank.

"Now you owe us *two,*" Sandy said.

"Okay," David said. "One: I think my father is a lousy architect."

"Boy, don't let *him* hear you say that."

"Well, isn't . . . ?"

"Of course," Sandy said.

"I mean, whatever we say here . . ."

"Naturally."

"So how can he hear it?"

"He won't hear it from *us,*" I said.

"Let's swear to that," Sandy said.

"Right, right."

"Whatever we say to each other . . ."

"*Whenever* we say it."

Sandy raised her eyes questioningly, waiting.

"I mean, not only now. *Whenever.*"

"Right, right, it's strictly between the three of us."

"I'll drink to that," David said, and drank.

"More truths," Sandy said.

"How many do I owe now?"

"How many does he owe, Peter?"

"Two."

"I'm almost out of beer," David said.

"Serum."

"Serum. Where's the serum opener?"

"Over there."

"Where?"

"Right there."

"Oh, good, good."

"Well, finish what you've got in the bottle first."

"Right," David said, and drank.

"That makes three," I said.

"You want them all in a row?"

"Yes."

"All in a row," Sandy said.

"Here goes," David said, and paused. "My mother has a boyfriend."

"How do you know?" Sandy asked, her eyes wide.

"I saw him."

"With *her?*"

"Yes."

"In *bed?*"

"Yes."

"Were they *doing* it?"

"Yep."

"When you came in?"

"I didn't *go* in," David said. "They didn't see me."

"Who *was* he?"

"I don't know."

"Where was your *father?*"

"In Chicago."

"Boy," I said.

"I walked around for maybe two hours," David said. "We were supposed to have a game that afternoon, you know, but it was called because the field was wet. Which is how I happened to get home early. So I walked around, and when I got back my mother asked me who won. I said we didn't play. She got this sort of panicky look on her face, you know, and her hand went up to her throat, like in some cheap television show, and she said 'Well, where *were* you all this time?' Just walking around, I said. And we looked at each other."

"Parents are a pain in the ass," Sandy said thoughtfully.

"Mmm," David said, and glanced through the opening in the poncho. It was raining harder now, the sky was blacker. "Where the hell's that opener?" he said. I tossed it to him, and he opened the second bottle of beer. "One of *you* go," he said, "I'm tired."

We were all very quiet. Outside, there was a streak of lightning, and then a thunderclap. I started biting my lip and wondering what I could tell them. I didn't want to tell them about the snot.

"Here's another truth for you," David said suddenly. "I once broke my grandfather's watch with a hammer, just smashed in the crystal. Then I threw it down the sewer, and when they asked me if I'd seen it, I said no."

"Why'd you do that?"

"I *wanted* to."

"But why?"

"Because he said there was a little man inside making it tick."

"Why'd he tell you a stupid thing like that?"

"Who knows? I was only four or five, he probably figured it would thrill me to know there was some little guy inside his watch. Instead, it scared hell out of me. That's why I smashed the watch and threw it down the sewer."

"But you didn't do it maliciously," Sandy said.

"Oh, *sure,* I did it maliciously," David said, and we all laughed.

"Whose turn is it?" Sandy said.

"I don't know," I said, and shrugged. I didn't want

to tell them about the snot, and yet it seemed to be the only thing I could think of.

"*You* go," Sandy said.

"No, go ahead, I'm thinking."

"Have some more beer," David said.

"Okay," I said, and drank.

Outside there was another flash of lightning. We held our breaths. The thunder came almost immediately, loud, close. A fresh torrent of rain beat noisily on the umbrella top.

"I . . ."

They both turned to look at me.

"Nothing," I said.

"Come on, don't be chicken," David said.

"No, I was just thinking."

"About what?"

"About . . ." I hesitated. "About Sandy's top."

"Oh, for Christ's sake," David said.

"What's wrong with that?" Sandy said. "He's supposed to tell the truth."

"That's right," I said, but I was lying, I hadn't been thinking about Sandy's top, I'd been thinking about the snot. Or maybe I'd been thinking about both.

"What *about* my top?" Sandy asked.

"Nothing," I said. I shrugged. "Just that it's wet, that's all."

"Would you like me to take it off?"

"No."

"Tell the truth. If you want me to take it off, I will."

"I don't know." I shrugged again. "David?"

"Oh, take the damn thing off if you want to," David said.

"Well, does *Peter* want me to?"

"Yeah, sure, go ahead," I said, "I don't care."

"It's not such a big deal, you know," Sandy said, and reached behind her to unclasp the bikini top. She put one hand into her sweatshirt, pulled out the top, and threw it on the blanket. "Oh, man," she said, "that feels a hundred percent better."

"Well, sure," David said, "we're not *kids* here."

"That's right," Sandy said, "we ought to get that straight."

"What do you mean?"

"Well, let's *really* be honest with each other all the time, okay?"

"Okay," I said.

"You're blushing."

"Am I?"

"Yes. Why?"

"I've never talked to a girl this way."

"I've never talked to a boy this way," Sandy said.

"So it's good," David said, and shrugged.

"Yes, it is," Sandy said. "I think it is."

"He's still blushing."

"No, I was thinking about something else."

"What?"

"Listen, are we really . . . I mean, it's never gonna go beyond the three of us, is it?"

"Of course not. If you ever told anyone I took off the top of my bathing suit . . ."

"Oh, come on, Sandy, why would we do that?"

"Well, boys sometimes . . ."

"Hey, come on, I thought this was something different."

"Well, it *is*."

"Then . . ."

"All right, I'm sorry," she said.

"Well, okay," David said.

"I *said* I was sorry."

"Either we trust each other or we don't," David said.

"I trust you both," Sandy said.

"Well, we trust you, too," David said.

"Yes, we do."

"Good," Sandy said, and we all drank again. "Tell us," she said to me.

"It's pretty disgusting."

"How bad can it be?"

"What'd you do?"

"Well, I made Ritz cracker sandwiches out of cream cheese and snot, and gave them to my cousin to eat."

David and Sandy both burst out laughing at the same time, surprising me. I'd thought they would kick me out of the tent or something, but instead they were laughing.

"Jesus, that's a *great* idea!" David said.

"Well, it was pretty disgusting," I said, but I was tremendously relieved.

"*I've* got a cousin I'd like to do that to," Sandy said, laughing.

"Only it wouldn't be *snot*," David said, and rolled over on the blanket laughing, knocking over a bottle of beer, and almost knocking down the umbrella and the poncho. Sandy and I jumped on him and began punching him on the back, and finally poured a full bottle of beer all over him.

We had each sneaked six-packs out of our respective refrigerators. We drank almost all the beer, and buried the rest in the sand, marking off the distance from a telephone pole with the number 7-381 on it on a small aluminum strip. It was still raining when we decided to go into the water. The beach was empty, the waves were still pounding in and dragging up a lot of muck. David and I took off our sweaters. I chased David into the water, and then we shouted for Sandy to come in.

"Just a second," she yelled from inside the poncho tent, and then she came out, still wearing her sweatshirt, and holding the top part of her suit in her hands. She looked out over the water, gave a shrug, and threw the top back inside. Then she pulled the sweatshirt

over her head, and came running down toward the
water, shrieking and yelling.

She had very small breasts.

I thought we did a very good job with the gull, if I
must say so myself.

To begin with, he turned out to be a very husky old
bird, ready to fly off long before the wound in his neck
had healed entirely. The day after Sandy got the collar
and leash on him, in fact, he fluttered out of his cardboard box, and immediately crouched over low, beak
thrust forward, wings back, like a swimmer about to
do a racing dive. He gave a sudden spring into the air,
opened his wings wide, flapped them wildly, got pulled
up short by the leash attached to the porch railing, and
came right down on his head. Gaining his feet again,
he looked at the three of us in a hurt, bewildered way,
and then gave it another try, going through the same
crouching routine, and the springing, and the flapping
and fluttering, this time squawking mightily and attracting the attention of several other gulls who
swooped low over the house and began squawking
back at him. Sandy and David and I sat on the porch
steps, watching as he got himself set for another try,
crouching, and then coming down the runway for a
takeoff and then going into his nosedive again when
the leash played out and the collar caught his throat.

I was beginning to think he was pretty stupid.

He must have tried it at least two dozen times before he began to get the feeling that *perhaps* something
was preventing him from taking off as was his usual
custom. The gulls circling the house lost interest (they
had probably thought food was involved and then realized there wouldn't be any handouts) and flew off. The
bird gazed at them wistfully, it seemed to me, and then
glared at the three of us where we sat quietly watching
him. Suspiciously, he looked up at the sky again, apparently thinking there was some sort of trick involved

here, some unseen force putting the whammie on him, and decided to dispense with his usual preparations for flight, surprising his invisible opponent instead by leaping into the air without a preliminary crouch. His new tactic earned him only another fall. He came crashing down quite hard this time. For a few minutes I figured he might have to go into surgery again, for the brain this time. But he staggered to his feet once more, looked balefully at us, and gave a squawk as if to say You bastards, what's the secret here, why can't I fly? Then he began pacing around the deck in the short circle proscribed by the length of the leash, took a cautious flutter up to the deck railing and actually pecked at the leash once or twice before trying to take off from his new perch—which only netted him another crashing blow to the cerebellum.

"He's gonna kill himself," David said.

"No, he'll catch on," Sandy answered.

I wasn't so sure.

To my surprise, though, the bird kept trying, seeming to gain a little more knowledge with each attempt, and at last learning that his own force being exerted against the leash was what snapped him back so fiercely each time. Once he understood the phenomenon, he ceased fighting the leash, and fluttered up tentatively to hover on the air instead, simply soared up quietly to the limit the leash allowed and then hung there and stared down at us with, it seemed to me, an altogether unwarranted look of smugness.

"I think he's got it," David said.

"By George, he's got it," I said.

Whereupon the bird dropped silently to the deck, tucked in his wings, walked to the box, gave a flying leap into it, squawked once, and hunched himself down into the paper scraps Sandy had arranged there for him.

"He's a smart old bird," Sandy said. "You'll see."

The very next day, the smart old bird zoomed up

out of his box again, almost broke his neck against the
restraining leash, and came crashing down to the hard
wooden floor of the deck. It seemed apparent to me
that he had a very short memory and an IQ of perhaps
60 or 70, but Sandy insisted he was the most brilliant
bird she had ever seen, and that it was only a matter of
time before he understood completely. I thought it
would only be a matter of time before he fractured his
skull. In fact, I think he managed to survive only because Sandy's mother began sounding off just then
about having a sea gull living in a cardboard box on
her sundeck and making a mess.

Sandy's mother was a divorcée, which meant that
she gave a lot of parties and entertained a lot of people, so I guess the gull *did* at first present a pretty
menacing picture, staring with an angry yellow eye
from the depths of his cardboard nest, like a phoenix
waiting to rise in anger, hardly the proper stimulus for
cocktail conversation. It began to be a regular melody
and counterpoint, as David described it, the gull bang-
ing his head on the deck and Sandy's mother in the
background nagging all the time, get rid of that horrid
old bird, get him off the porch, he frightens my friends,
look at the mess he's making, and so on.

We had seen some of the friends Sandy's mother
dragged out to the island, however, and it was our
opinion—all three of us—that if the gull succeeded in
scaring off even a few of them, he'd be performing a
great service. The one we particularly disliked, and
whom we cut up with regularity every Monday afternoon (he usually spent the weekend and left by heli-
copter early Monday morning) was a lawyer who had
an office on Pine Street downtown. He was a tubby little man who always wore a white tee shirt over his
bathing suit, even when he went into the water. "I
have very fair skin," he told anyone who would listen,
"I turn lobster red in the sun." It was Sandy's opinion
that Snow White, as we called him, was sleeping with

her mother, and the thought nauseated all of us, Sandy especially. He had a habit of saying "Point of fact" before he began a statement, regardless of whether what he as about to say was really fact. "Point of fact," he would say, "most people dislike turnips," or something equally stupid. He drank martinis made only with Booth's gin; Sandy's mother kept a bottle especially for him. He hated the gull. When we first began our training program, we toyed with the idea of teaching the bird to bite him. On the ass was where we had in mind.

But because of the pressure from Sandy's mother, we finally moved the bird from the deck to the back of the house, which didn't turn out too badly after all. There was a shed back there which was used for storing the garbage cans. Since the bird would eat practically anything we tossed him, it was very convenient being so close to the garbage cans. What we did was drill a hole near the top of a piece of lead pipe and then put a long bolt through the hole, making a crosspiece around which we could loop the end of the gull's leash. Then we sank three feet of the pipe into the sand near the shed, leaving six or seven inches exposed.. Sandy was afraid the bird would be smart enough (a premise I seriously doubted) to figure out how to lift the leash off the cross bolt. David, however, insisted that this was the only way to tether a bird, he naturally having tethered thousands and thousands of birds in his life, so Sandy accepted his judgment, and the training began in earnest.

The gull was much happier with his new surroundings. If you are the type of stupid bird who keeps landing on your head, it's better by a long shot to have a sand pile to practice on, rather than a wooden deck. Eventually, of course, the leash made its point. The gull was a captive, and he realized it at last and became the first walking bird in the history of America. In fact, Sandy got him to the point where he was almost heeling, though most of the time he just strutted along either ahead or behind. Every now and then, he'd try to take off, forgetting that he wasn't supposed to fly. But Sandy would give a short sharp snap of the leash, and he'd come back down, squawking a little (he was really a cantankerous old crank) but walking along nonetheless, and waiting for his reward from the small bag of garbage one or the other of us always carried.

We even took him out on the sailboat several times, though the sight of him tied to a deck cleat, staring into the wind, his feathers bristling, always gave me a funny feeling. As though he were an old Greek slave who had been captured by the Romans, faithful to them, but always pining for Athens or someplace. That was the feeling I got whenever I watched him on the deck of the boat, peering into the wind with his yellow eyes.

The boat belonged to my father, but he let us use her whenever we wanted to, except on weekends. She was a fiber-glass auxiliary, a twenty-footer with a mainsail and jib. There were two berths in the cabin, and the cockpit—more than six feet long—provided sleeping accommodations for another two as well. There was a built-in icebox and a concealed head, a sink, and a water tank, a hanging locker and an outboard in a well, an enclosed motor compartment and a canvas dodger that provided full headroom in the galley. She was a nice little boat, and we probably used her more often than my father did that summer. Between the day of the truth serum and the day David got grounded—that was a full week—we had the boat out four times, which was an awful lot considering we were trying to train a bird at the same time.

The boat was moored at the island marina, a combination boatel with twelve cottages, run by a very fat flamboyant old lady who wore pendant earrings even in the morning. Her name was Violet, and she was al-

ways surrounded by a lot of fags; David's father called
her the Queen Bee. She had orange hair, and she wore
white makeup; she truly was a pretty frightening old
dame. But she also knew a lot about boats, and once
she helped me locate and repair a broken spring in the
engine.

The three of us—four, counting the gull—would go
down to the marina early in the morning, stow our
gear in the cockpit, buy whatever supplies we needed
from Violet, and then go out under power until we hit
open water. David and I would then hoist the sails, and
off we'd go, skimming the water. Sandy sitting in the
stern in a bikini, the wooden tiller tucked under her
slender arm, her eyes the color of the blue fiber-glass
hull, her grin cracking wide across her face. Sometimes
we'd furl the sails and just let the boat drift, lying on
deck and soaking up sun, David's transistor radio
tuned to ABC, or sometimes QXR. He was a music
major at Music and Art, and he played the flute like
an angel, both jazz and classical, but he very rarely
foisted long-hair music on us, and usually we just listened to Ron Lundy or Dan Ingram or one of the
other great disk jockeys. The gull would give a squawk
every now and then, and Sandy would lazily say, "Oh,
shut up, bird," and then roll over to get the sun on her
back. We had snorkels and fins and masks, and whenever we found a little cove where the water seemed
brighter than the rest of the Sound, we'd go over the
side looking for crabs and small fish, but there really
wasn't very much to see.

It was Violet who suggested we try an island some
six miles due north of Greensward. She had started
selling us six-packs even though it was against the law.
I think she had her eye on David. She always used to
put her arm around his shoulder when we came in, or
stand close to him with her enormous hanging breasts
pressed against his arm. David complained that he had
never met a more repulsive woman in his life, and he

pointed out something we had missed about her, the
fact that she smelled of pumpkin.

"Have you ever cleaned out the insides of a pumpkin on Halloween," he said, "the smell of the gooky
seedy pulp inside? That's what Violet smells like when
you get close to her."

David was the first one to notice this, of course, because she always seemed to be standing closest to *him,*
but once he told us about it, we got the whiff, too. I
thought it was disgusting and surmised it was from
hanging around with fags, because they all wear the
same secret perfume that goes out on the air to other
fags everywhere, the way some species of animals send
out musk. Anyway, Violet smelled like a pumpkin, and
she liked David very much, and because of him she
sold us beer on the sneak. We had to go around to the
back door for it. We usually took only two six-packs
with us when we went out on the boat. It is very easy
to get bombed out of your mind, and on a sailboat it's
important to know what you're doing at all times.

On this one morning in the third week of July, the
four of us marched around to Violet's marina—the of-
ficial name of the place was The Blue Grotto—and
Sandy and I waited out front while David went around
back to get the beer. We were surprised to see Violet
because she usually made it her business to be where-
ever David was, but this morning she popped out of
the front screen door, smelling of pumpkin as usual,
and asked us if we had heard about this delightful little
island six miles due north. Violet had a way of using
words one usually associated with tiny women. She
must have weighed a hundred and eighty pounds, and
she wore flowered muu muus that made her look even
bigger, but she was always using words like "delicious"
and "cunning" and "charming" that made you think of
a smaller person.

We told her we hadn't heard of the island, and she
went inside and came back with a C.&G.S. chart of the

area (which we had aboard the boat, anyway) and pointed out a small island shaped like a fishhook.

"You've got a good wind today," she said, "you could make it in little more than an hour."

It was my guess we could make it in much less than that, but I didn't say anything.

"What's so special about it?" Sandy asked, and the gull on his leash squawked, and she said, "Oh, shut up, bird."

"I saw you going aboard with snorkeling equipment the other day," Violet said. "There's some divine snorkeling there."

"Well, maybe we'll give it a try," I said.

"If you'd like me to navigate . . ." Violet started, and I quickly said, "Thanks, Vi, but that won't be necessary."

"Because I've been there, you know, and I could help you find it."

"Well," I said, tactfully, I thought, "we've got this identical chart aboard, and I'm sure we can find it without any trouble at all. But thanks a lot."

"Be sure you go in through the channel," Violet said.

"We'll be very careful," I promised.

David came around the corner of the boatel just then, with the two six-packs wrapped in his poncho.

"What's up?" he said.

"Good morning, David," Violet said, and moved over close to him with her pumpkin aroma.

"We're going to try this new island," Sandy said.

"I'll come along if you want me to," Violet said, and smiled at David.

"Gee, thanks a lot, Vi," David said, "but that won't be necessary."

"Do the two of you always give the same answers?" Violet asked.

"The *three* of us," Sandy corrected.

"Thanks a lot, though, Vi," David called over his shoulder, and we all went down to the boat.

It was a gorgeous day, sunny and hot—I had to take off my sweatshirt—but there was a nice breeze, too, and not a cloud in the sky. Standing on the deck of the boat in surfing trunks and a floppy blue hat, I could see for miles and miles, everything so sharp and clear and true, the mainsail billowing out in a good strong wind, David leaning on the cockpit in his white tennis shorts, Sandy at the tiller in a lacy bikini and a straw hat with ragged edges, we were some motley crew. The gull, tethered to his usual cleat just aft of the cockpit, was staring into the wind the way he always did, squawking every now and then, to which Sandy every now and then would say, "Oh, shut up, bird."

We found the island without any trouble.

The channel was clearly marked on our chart, and it showed a depth of seven feet in the center, which was fine since the boat had a draft of three feet with the stick down. We anchored close in, and Sandy and I put on the masks and fins and jumped over. The bird gave a little squawk as we went over the side, and David told him to shut up. David had opened a can of beer and was serving as lookout.

There wasn't much to see down there. I was beginning to think Violet had made up the whole snorkeling thing in the hope we'd ask her to come along. Sandy and I dove for about a half hour, and then David went in with her, but all any of us saw were a couple of crabs and some eels, and the usual quota of beer bottles and sneakers and junk. We lay around on deck in the sun afterward, and then had our lunch and decided to explore the island. We left the bird tethered to his cleat, and swam in.

The beach was flat and pebbly where we came ashore, a dune rising up behind it, covered with beach plum and grass. A fisherman's net, gray and stiff and rotted, hung over the skeleton of a beached rowboat. The charred remains of a fire were near the bow of the boat. A beer can was half-buried in the sand near the fire.

"When we find him," David said, crouching near the ashes, "we'll have to give him a name."

"What's today?" Sandy asked.

"Monday."

"Too bad," she said, and clucked her tongue.

We climbed the dune behind the boat and saw that the island fell away sharply to the south, the land low and dotted with marshes that reflected the sun in a hundred different places, as though someone had spilled a handful of gold coins onto the ground. At the far end of the island, there was a stand of towering pines in dark-green silhouette against the sky.

"It's a nice island," Sandy said.

"Mmm."

"Want to walk it a little?"

"Sure."

We half-expected to run across someone, I suppose, but we didn't. The fire near the boat could have been cold for an hour or a day or a week, there was no telling. Traces of humanity were scattered all over the island, though, and it was funny to keep discovering evidence of people without seeing any of the people themselves.

After a while, Sandy said, "We're Martians who've just landed in a spaceship, and we have no idea what human beings are like. All we can do is reconstruct them from their artifacts."

Then she stooped to pick up a rusty spoon, and a speculated that the people on earth were undoubtedly only a foot high, otherwise why would their shovels be so small? Later, when we found a pair of tattered madras swimming trunks, I said they corrobrated Sandy's theory since this was obviously a shirt for a creature with a very small chest, and then went on to speculate

that earthlings had two heads since there were two
neckholes in the garment. But the game was exceed-
ingly difficult to play, and we gave it up after only a
few more tries. Linking hands, we shrieked and ran
down a sharply sloping, loosely packed stretch of sand
that led directly into the pine forest.

It was cool and dark under the trees. I felt, I can't
explain it, I felt a sudden gladness sweep over me, as
though my heart were expanding unbearably inside my
chest. The forest echoed with life, its luxuriant growth
seemed to reach out to me and absorb me so that I felt
like a growing thing myself, grasping for the sun. I
gripped Sandy's hand more tightly.

"Listen," I said.

"I don't hear anything," she answered.

"Listen to everything."

"Neither do I," David said.

Sandy suddenly pulled her hand away, frowned, and
said, "This is creepy."

"Let's get the hell out of here," David said.

They turned and swiftly walked away from me. I
could hear the surf far away, the repetition of an in-
sect's song, the gentle soughing of the wind in the treetops. I hesitated only a moment longer and then I followed them.

That night, David got grounded.

This was a full week after the rainy afternoon with
the truth serum, and I really thought it was senseless
to punish David for something he had done a week before. Besides, when you considered the element of
chance involved, the retroactive grounding seemed
even more idiotic: if Mr. Porter hadn't sent his bill on
the fifteenth and charged David's mother twice for the
beer, she never would have found out at all. I was dis-
gusted with the whole concept.

The preceding Monday we had each sneaked six-
packs of beer out of our refrigerators, this being before

we'd made our working arrangement with Violet. Because of the peculiar circular design of David's house, the storage space was severely limited (not to mention the fact that you couldn't place anything flush against the curved and sloping walls—maybe David's father *was* a lousy architect). So instead of putting one carton of beer in the refrigerator to chill, the way most people do, leaving the spare cartons in the pantry or the closet, in David's house they would order three six-packs every week and stick all three in the refrigerator. David's mother always shopped on Saturday, and the truth serum business took place on Monday, and the very next day she noticed that there were only two cartons of beer in the refrigerator instead of three. In fact, there were exactly seven bottles of beer, since David's father had drunk a few between Saturday and Tuesday, so that was when the first call to Mr. Porter took place. The first call, as it was later revealed, went something like this. David's mother told Mr. Porter that she was certain he had delivered only *two* cartons of beer instead of three because here it was only Tuesday and they hadn't had any weekend guests and yet there were only seven bottles of beer in the refrigerator. Mr. Porter said he had made up the order himself and distinctly remembered putting *three* six-packs into it, but he would nonetheless send his boy over with an additional carton and, of course, would not charge her for it. So on the following Monday, David's mother got the bill and, instead of Mr. Porter *not* charging her for the additional six-pack, he *had* charged her—and he a millionaire. So David's mother made the second phone call to Mr. Porter, telling him that he had made a mistake with his bill, and going over the entire incident again, while meanwhile David and Sandy and I were exploring Violet's island and drinking the beer Violet had sold us.

Mr. Porter calmly explained to David's mother that yes, he *had* charged her for the extra carton of beer

because upon checking further, he remembered something about the order but had not had a chance to call
her back. What he remembered was that he'd had only
three cartons of Heineken (David's father's brand) in
stock when he'd gone to the refrigerator, which fact
had caused him to write a memo to reorder, which
memo was now in front of him, would David's mother
care to have him read it to her on the phone? Yes, David's mother said. Very well, Mr. Porter said, Reorder
Heineken Beer, and it's dated Saturday, July the
eighth, and right here in the corner are my wife's ini-
tials, MJP for Mary Jane Porter, meaning she has already taken care of the reordering. So that's how I
know I gave you *three* cartons and not *two,* and that's
why I charged you for the extra one I sent over, which
you may have noticed was Löwenbräu and not Heineken, because the Heineken still hasn't come in yet.
Thank you, David's mother said, and hung up.

She then, naturally, called in the maid, whose name
was Eudice, and asked her whether she remembered
how many cartons of beer she'd put into the refrigerator last Saturday when the order came from Mr. Porter's—was it two or three? Eudice, who was raised in
North Carolina, and who had difficulty counting past
the number five, examined her fingers and told David's
mother that she had put three cartons in the refrigerator, and then went on with amazing if not total recall
to itemize the exact number of times David's father
had gone to the refrigerator for beer, as for example
the two bottles he had drunk with the barbecued spare-
ribs they'd had that Saturday night, and the one he'd
had on Sunday afternoon after fixing the water pump,
and the two he'd had with those funny clam things—

The marinated clams, David's mother said.

—yes, on Sunday night, Eudice went on. As a matter of fact, she herself had been surprised last Monday,
what with it raining so hard and all, to find only a car-

ton and a little bit more of beer, instead of there being *two* cartons and a little bit more.

When did you discover this? David's mother naturally asked.

It was just after your son left the house, Eudice the rat answered.

So that's what was waiting for David when he stepped through the door after the day on Violet's island. His father went through the outraged older party routine, the shame of learning that his own son was drinking behind his back, what *other* things was David doing that his father knew nothing about? Are you smoking, too? he asked, *are* you?

David denied drinking, he denied smoking, he almost denied breathing. If only you had *asked,* his mother said, we would have *given* you the beer (which was a bald-faced lie). But no, you had to *steal* it, oh David, I'm so ashamed of you, and so on, as if she had just cracked the Brinks robbery.

So they grounded him.

For three days.

The grounding was a full-dress one, too. He wasn't permitted to leave the house, of course, but neither was he permitted to have friends there or to talk to them on the telephone. He was allowed only one phone call (as soon as he hung up, Sandy said to me, "Do you think we should get him a lawyer?"), which was how he managed to let us know what had happened. All in all, it looked as though a desolate few days lay ahead.

The first day was very difficult.

We had gone out to the point on Tuesday morning, searching for our cache of beer near the telephone pole with the aluminum strip marked 7-382 on it, and practically digging up half the beach until we remembered we'd buried it at the foot of 7-381. We unearthed two bottles and carried them into the tall beach grass because there were some other kids around, and also

some adults playing volleyball without a net. Sandy
took the bottle opener out of her bikini top, removed
the Kleenex she had wrapped it in, opened both bottles, said, "Here's to the prisoner of Zenda," meaning
David, winked, drank, and then reached into her canvas beach bag for what looked like a railroad time-
table.

"Did you see this?" she asked, and handed it to me.

The brochure was perhaps eight inches long and
three inches wide, folded in half lengthwise and then in
half again. It was printed in blue ink. The headline
read: INTRODUCING SELECTA-DATE.

"What is it?" I said.

"Read it."

I read it quickly. The first page explained that this
was a new scientific method of meeting people who
were specifically suited to one's own tastes and needs,
all of it made possible through the modern miracle of
electronic data processing. It went on to explain that
the answers to this questionnaire (which comprised the
remaining pages of the folder) would be fed into a
computer programmed to discover "that perfect date
who will complement your personality, your likes and
dislikes, your outlooks and ideals, your physical
tastes."

"What do you think?" Sandy asked.

"What do *you* think?" I answered.

"I think we ought to screw up the machine," Sandy
said.

I'd noticed that a registration fee of ten dollars was
required for each applicant, and I immediately wondered whether it was worth that much to screw up a
machine. She saw my hesitancy and said, "What's the
matter?"

"It costs ten bucks to join," I said.

"That's only a little more than three dollars each,"
Sandy said. "David'll go along with it, don't you
think?"

"I don't know." I hesitated again. "I wish he was here."

"I do, too. Let's fill it out, Peter. Just for fun. We don't have to mail it in if we don't want to."

"Okay," I said.

We sipped a little more beer. Sandy took a ballpoint pen from her beach bag, and propped the folder on a copy of *McCall's,* which she supported with her knees. It was a very hot day. A fine sheen of sweat was on her chest above the bikini top. I thought fleetingly of that day she'd run into the water naked above the waist. Sandy immediately said, "What?"

"Nothing."

"Peter," she said warningly.

"I was thinking of the day you went in the water without your top," I admitted.

"Oh, yeah," she said, and grinned. "Some show, huh?"

"Well, *I* think it was," I said, and shrugged.

"Shall we fill this thing out or not?" she said.

"Yeah, sure, let's fill it out."

The first question (as indeed the entire first *page* of questions) was multiple choice, the applicant being asked to circle his or her age bracket. Since the youngest bracket listed was 17–19, Sandy was clearly ineligible to begin with. But in order to screw up the machine, she circled the listing for 20–22. I was still thinking about that day, and was getting a little annoyed by her refusal to discuss it. We'd promised to tell the truth at all times, hadn't we? So why had she just brushed me off? She went down the questionnaire now, reading the questions and the choices out loud, circling her height as 5'3" to 5'5", a good two inches less than her real height, and then describing herself as "of ample build." She claimed to have a masters degree, black hair, and blue eyes—she did have blue eyes, of course. But she further claimed to be Oriental, *and* Jewish, *and* fluent in Chinese and Greek, *and* Republican in outlook.

She then came to a question that asked whether she considered herself Very Bright, Bright, or Average, and immediately circled Very Bright. Since I was annoyed, anyway, I coughed politely and looked up at the sky.

"I *am*," she said. "I have an IQ of 157." She lowered her eyes. "I'm sorry, that sounds like boasting. Shall I cross it out and circle Bright instead?"

"Do what you want to do," I said. I couldn't stop thinking about that day last week, and I blamed *her* for what I was thinking, figuring if she'd only *discuss* the damn thing, we could forget it. At the same time, I was embarrassed by the memory of how she'd looked, and ashamed of myself for feeling so horny. Finally, I blamed David for having stupidly got himself grounded, though I couldn't really imagine what that had to do with any of it.

"Should my date be Negro, Caucasian, or Oriental?" Sandy asked.

"Negro," I said.

"No, let's say Puerto Rican. That'll *really* screw 'em up."

"Is there a listing for Puerto Rican?"

"No, I'll write it in."

"Okay," I said. My mouth was dry.

"Peter, what the hell *is* it?"

"Well, if you really want to know," I said, "I was pretty interested that day."

"What day?"

"The day you took off your top."

"Oh," Sandy said.

"If you *really* want to know," I said, "which I guess you don't."

"Sure I do," she said. "I appreciate your telling me, I do, Peter."

"Thanks."

"It's perfectly all right that you were interested. I don't mind."

"I'm glad you don't mind."

"In fact, I'm flattered."

"Yeah, well."

"I mean, I'm so little, Peter," she said, and laughed. Nervously, it seemed to me.

"You're not so little," I said.

"Thank you, Peter," she said, "that's very sweet of you." She hesitated, and then smiled and said, "Shall we finish this?" and tapped the questionnaire with the tip of her pen.

"No, I want to settle this other thing first."

"But what's there to . . ." she started, and then turned to stare at me.

"It's still on my mind," I said.

"Oh, come on, Peter."

"Well, we promised to tell the truth, and that's the truth."

"Well . . . I . . ." She gave a brief puzzled shrug. "Well . . . well, what about it?"

"I want you to do it again."

"Do *what*? Take off my *top*?"

"Yes," I said, and swallowed, and looked away from her.

"Oh, boy," she said.

"Well, that's the truth. That's what's on my mind, and that's the truth."

"Oh, boy," she said again.

"Well," I said, and was silent.

Sandy stared at me. "There are people around," she said at last.

"Yeah."

"I'd take it off if there weren't."

"Sure."

We were silent again.

"You don't believe me," Sandy said.

"I believe you."

"Peter, it doesn't mean a thing to me. I'd take it off in a minute if we were alone."

"Sure."

"I would."

I did not answer her. She began tapping the pen on the magazine cover. Down on the beach I could hear the volleyball players shouting.

"I just don't understand you," I said at last, shaking my head. "Didn't you know David and I would . . ." I shrugged.

"No, I didn't."

"Well, what'd you *expect?*"

"I don't know, but I didn't once think you'd . . ." She shook her head angrily. "We can't even *talk* straight anymore, see what you did?"

"*I* can talk straight," I said.

"Oh, sure." She picked up a tiny beach shell and, studying it, said, "Did . . . did David, too?"

"How would I know?"

"Didn't you discuss it with him?"

"Behind your back?" I said, shocked.

"I thought . . ."

"Of *course* not!"

"Peter, you're getting me very confused."

"It's just that I don't know what's supposed to *happen* here."

"Happen?"

"Yes, *between* us."

"Between us?"

"Jesus, Sandy, must you repeat . . . ?"

"I don't understand you, damn it. I don't *understand!*"

"Are we supposed to . . . are David and I supposed to . . . to . . ."

"What?"

"Do things?"

"No," she said immediately.

"Then . . . then what do you *expect* us to do, if you take off your top like that?"

"Nothing."

"Then why'd you do it?"

"Because . . . because I didn't think it would matter, one way or the other."

"Well, it got me excited," I said quickly, and turned away in embarrassment.

"Well, I don't know what to do about that," Sandy said.

"Well, I don't know, either."

"If you're going to be thinking about my *breasts* all the goddamn time . . ."

"I don't think about them *all* the goddamn time. I just happen to be thinking about them *now*." In defense, I said, "That bikini's hardly anything at all."

"Well, then, I'll just stop wearing bikinis, that's all."

"Everybody wears bikinis."

"Then go think about *them* a little."

"I never saw *them* without their tops."

"And you won't ever see *me* again, either!" she said angrily, and threw the shell into her beach bag.

"I thought you said . . ."

"Never mind what I said, the *hell* with what I said."

"Okay."

"Okay." She was silent for a long time. I kept wondering why she didn't get up and walk away. I dreaded the thought of facing David. How could I possibly tell him about this?

"If only we could . . ." she started, and then shook her head. "I thought you understood," she said.

"I do."

"No, you don't," she said, and fell silent again. She was thoughtful for a long time. Then she sighed and put the magazine and the questionnaire and the pen into her beach bag. She rose, tugged at the bikini pants, adjusted the bikini top, brushed sand from her thighs, and held out her hand to me. For a moment she stood against the sun and was faceless.

I looked up at her and tried to see her eyes.

"Come," she said.

I took her hand, and she pulled me to my feet. I felt very clumsy. I felt I should apologize to her. We began walking. We walked in silence, the beach bag hanging from her shoulder, thudding against her thigh with every step she took. The sun was hot. We were climbing up and away from the beach. The sound of the volleyball game was far behind us now. We continued to climb. I realized suddenly that we were heading toward the center of the island, where the fire had been.

"Listen," I said, "let's forget it." Inexplicably, I had begun trembling.

"No," she said.

"Sandy . . ."

"I *want* you to see me," she said. "Don't be afraid."

"I'm not."

"Peter, you're lying."

"All right, I *am* afraid."

"Of what?"

"That I'll do something to you."

"You won't."

"How do you know?"

"I won't let you."

We were approaching the forest. The burnt pines were gnarled and black against the sky. I was trembling violently now.

"It's too open," I said, "they'll see us."

"Who?" she asked.

"I don't know. I feel . . ."

"No one will see us," she said.

We found a huge boulder, as black as the skeletal trees surrounding it. Still trembling, I sat with my back to it on the side away from the distant ocean. Sandy stood before me silently and solemnly, and reached behind her to unclasp the top of the suit. Her nipples looked exactly the way they had that day she'd rushed into the water, that day the icy water touched them.

She smiled and sat down beside me. Then she reached into the beach bag again, and began filling out the questionnaire, reading the questions and possible answers aloud to me.

Eventually, I stopped trembling.

The fire, of course, had taken place long before I was born. The way it was told to me, it had started in the only house on the edge of the forest, a modern structure with sliding screens and a wide deck that faced the rising sun. The man and woman living there had been having trouble for a good many years, constantly threatening divorce, even coming to blows one night in public at The Blue Grotto. On the night of the fire, they'd had a terrible argument, and the man had seized the nearest object at hand, a lighted kerosene lamp, and thrown it at his wife. Her nylon gown had gone up in flames. Shrieking in terror, she had raced outdoors, dropping tatters of fire into the adjacent brush. It had been a dry summer, and there was a high wind that night. The flames leaped from bush to bush, eventually reaching the forest itself, where the wilting pines supplied fresh fuel for the blaze. The summer people stood in panic on the beach, watching the flames billow up into the sky, a dense black cloud of smoke hanging over the forest, the strong wind and the flying sparks threatening to spread the fire everywhere. The only thing that saved the island was a sudden crosswind that turned the flames back upon themselves.

Before that day with Sandy, I could never think of that ancient fire without scaring myself. Whenever the wind was unusually high, I would look southward from the back porch of our house and visualize those billowing flames, that hanging black cloud, the slender woman rushing in terror through the brush. Oh yes, the islanders had since built a firehouse and supplied it with a shining engine and a siren that could be heard all the way over on the mainland. And yes, there was a volunteer fire department now, and everyone had been alerted to and understood the possible danger. But it had happened once, and my constant fear was that it might happen again—and this time no lucky crosswind would spring up to prevent a total holocaust. The fear was unrealistic, I guess, but that didn't make it any less frightening. On particularly anxious days, I would find myself hating those long-ago people who had allowed such a thing to happen. Why did *I* have to tremble now for something they had been unable to prevent? Why did I even have to consider the *possibility* of another fire?

And then, the day Sandy sat beside me, everything seemed suddenly all right. Smiling encouragement, inviting me to look and admire, she forced from my mind all previous knowledge of that horrible place. There beside her, I was able to dismiss the evidence of devastation all around me and consider the fire a legend passed from generation to generation (Have you heard of the terrible fire of '45, horrible, we hope and pray it will never happen here again), but *only* a legend. Besides, legend or not, we'd had nothing to do with that ancient fire—and so, guiltless, we could sit in the sunshine with the burnt and stunted trees all around us, secure in the knowledge that what we did now was also quite innocent: Sandy showed me her breasts. That was all. So, we concerned ourselves only with the present. The present was figuring out the answers to a questionnaire that would later be electronically computerized in an attempt to find the perfect date for Sandy. The present was Sandy herself sitting half-naked beside me in the ruins of the forest.

When David was finally sprung and we told him what had happened, he agreed with us that we'd done nothing wrong, and said he was only sorry he hadn't been there. In fact, he said, hadn't we all seen at least that much in the pages of *Playboy?* This was a point neither Sandy nor I had considered before. We agreed now that there was great validity to it, and immediately stopped arguing the morality of what had happened. In dismissal, Sandy mentioned that she'd also seen a picture of the highly respectable Countess Christina Paolozzi in *Vogue,* naked to the waist, "and she has even smaller breasts than mine, so there," she said, and stuck out her tongue. We all laughed and said the hell with it.

Besides, we had already embarked on a new project.

The day after David was sprung, Sandy came up with an idea for the further training of the gull. It seemed to her that since it had been so easy (ha!) to leash-train the bird, it should be even simpler to teach him something for which he had a natural talent, namely, to fly over our heads wherever we went.

"That's impossible," I said.

"It can be done," Sandy said.

"Not even with a homing pigeon, which he isn't."

"It can be done," Sandy insisted. "And if you won't help me, I'll just have to do it alone."

"Here comes the damsel-in-distress routine," David said, and rolled his eyes.

"Well, why do I always have to *beg* you?" Sandy said.

"Where's your violin, David?" I said.

"What key shall I play it in?"

"You're both louses," Sandy said.

We bought a fifty-foot reel of ten-pound nylon fishline, and fastened one end of it to the metal loop in the bird's collar. Then we led him out to the point, where we figured there would be fewer distractions than anywhere else on the island—except perhaps the forest—and fastened the other end of the line to a heavy piece of driftwood partially submerged in the sand. The bird didn't know what we wanted at first. We all kept running up to him and fluttering our hands at him and shouting, "Shoo, bird!" or "Let's go, bird!" but he was so used to our antics and our presence that he merely sat unblinkingly in the sand without so much as rustling a feather.

"He thinks we're crazy," I said.

"We *are* crazy," David said.

Sandy walked over to where the bird was calmly observing us. She put her hands on her hips and stood over him menacingly. "Listen, bird," she said, "we want you to fly."

"That's it," David said, "talk to him. You're sure to get results that way."

"Just shut up, David," she said, without turning. "You hear me, bird? You're going to fly."

"He hears you," David said.

"David, I'm warning you."

"You hear her, bird?"

"Come on, you damn bird," Sandy said, and picked him up in both hands and threw him violently into the air. The gull took wing for just an instant, more a braking action than anything else, and then gently fluttered back to the sand again.

"We'll have to take turns," Sandy said.

"Doing what?"

"Throwing him up."

"Look, Ma, I'm throwing up a sea gull," David said.

"David, today you're obnoxious," Sandy said.

"I know."

"Well, try not to be."

"I can't help it. I've been without you for too long a time."

"Oh, boy," Sandy said.

"It's true."

"Yeah," Sandy said, and walked over to the bird again. Crouching beside him in the sand, she very softly said, "Listen, bird, I'm going to keep tossing you up in the air until you start flying, you hear me?"

"I hear you," David answered in a high falsetto voice.

Sandy picked up the bird. "Here we go," she said, and flung him into the air. But he only spread his wings in the earlier braking motion, and drifted down to the ground again.

"He's the same brilliant bird he always was," I said, and David laughed.

"You're a lot of help," Sandy said.

"What do *you* think, Wilbur?" I said.

"Orville, you'll never get that crate off the ground," David answered.

"You're both hilarious," Sandy said. She walked over to the gull again. "Bird," she said, "you're getting me sore."

"You're frightening me," David said in his falsetto.

"You are going to fly," he said.

"Yes, missie," David said.

"Up *there*," Sandy said, and pointed. The gull actually followed her finger; it almost seemed he understood. But when she threw him into the air again, he merely braked and came back down to earth.

We all walked over to him. He looked up at us.

"He's a goddamn stupid idiot," Sandy said.

We stood around him in a circle. I think he was a little frightened. Then—I don't know who it was—*one* of us suddenly realized we were being watched, and we all turned together to look at the dune behind us. A girl with dark hair was silently standing there. From a distance, she seemed to be about eighteen years old. She was wearing a bottle-green, one-piece bathing suit. She had full breasts and a chunky figure. Her head was tilted to one side as she squinted into the sun. One hand was on her hip, the other rested on the opposite thigh.

"What are you doing to that bird?" she called.

"None of your business," Sandy called back.

The girl gave a brief nod, and then started down the

dune, her heels digging in as she slid toward the beach. She walked toward us purposefully, without any sense of urgency, a steady short-legged stride, her head bent, nodding all the while, as though she had decided to take some sort of action and was now priming herself to perform it. She stopped about three feet from where we were standing, put both hands on her hips, looked up at us, and said, "You'd better leave that bird alone."

"He happens to be *my* bird," Sandy said.

"That doesn't give you the license to treat him cruelly," the girl said.

Sandy looked at me, and I looked at David, and then the three of us looked at the girl. She was still facing the sun, her eyes squinted, her nose wrinkled, her mouth lopsided, her entire face screwed up in defense against its glare. She was very white, almost as white as the Pine Street lawyer. She had bands on her upper teeth, and they glinted in the sunshine now as she curled her lip in what I suppose she thought was a fierce manner. Up close, she looked about sixteen or so. She had freckles across her nose and on her cheeks. They seemed strangely out of place on a girl with such dark hair.

"Well?" she said.

"Go lose yourself," David said.

"Not until you take that collar off the bird," the girl said. She folded her arms across her chest. We all looked at each other again. Sandy sighed. I put one finger in my ear. David started nodding his head, short little nods.

"Are you going to leave that bird alone," the girl said, "or do I have to report this to the police?"

"You go report it to the police," I said.

"Yeah, you go do that."

"You go suck your mother's tit," Sandy said, and the girl's eyes opened wide for just an instant. Blinded by the sun's sudden assault, she turned her head aside and then backed a few paces away from us.

"Go on," Sandy said, "get out of here."

"It's a free country," the girl answered.

"This is a private beach," Sandy said.

"It *is* not. *None* of this beach is private, it's all dedicated to the public."

"Go to hell," Sandy said. To us, she said, "Let's get back to the bird."

"Over my dead body,'" the girl said.

Sandy gave her a penetrating look, and she backed off another few paces. The contrast between the two of them was really startling. This was almost the end of July, and Sandy was deeply tanned by then, her hair much blonder than it had been at the beginning of the summer, her blue eyes more vivid, a tiny dazzling tent-like wedge of white showing where her upper lip curled away from her teeth. There was about her a look of lean suppleness, a fluid, long-legged nonchalance in the way she stood or moved. The other girl, standing behind Sandy and perhaps six feet away from her, looked like a distorted funhouse mirror image, reflecting back in negative. Where Sandy was blond, the other girl was dark. Where Sandy's hair was long and loose, hers was cut close to her head, settling about her ears and the back of her neck like a cast-iron kettle. Her eyes, visible now that she was standing with her back to the sun and had opened them wide, were a deep brown, almost as dark as her hair. She gave the impression of being many years older than Sandy, of being in fact almost middle-aged, with large maiden-aunt breasts, and a clipped no-nonsense voice. I think we all felt a little strange around her. Not because she objected to what we were trying to teach the bird, but only because she seemed like a goddamn grownup.

She stood in spread-legged chunkiness now, her arms folded across her chest, as Sandy picked up the

bird again and flung him into the air. She watched as
the bird opened his wings, braked, and came down to
the sand again. She made no comment until Sandy had
tried the same thing unsuccessfully three times in a
row. Then she said, "What is it you're trying to do?"

Sandy didn't answer.

"What's she trying to do?" she asked David.

"Train him," David said briefly.

"To do what?"

"To fly."

"Doesn't he *know* how to fly?"

"Of course he knows how to fly," Sandy snapped.

"It's just that he's *forgotten* how to fly," I said.

"A bird cannot forget how to fly," the girl said. "It's
instinctive."

"What are you, an ornithologist?" David said.

"No, but I have a canary."

"This bird has been walking for a long time, you
see," I said.

"That makes no difference."

"He also happens to be a very dumb bird," I said.

"He's very *bright,*" Sandy said.

"Yes, he's very bright," I said, "but he's forgotten
how to fly."

"Perhaps he prefers walking," the girl said.

"Who asked you?" Sandy said.

"I'm merely offering an opinion."

"We don't need opinions," Sandy said.

"Yeah, why don't you get lost?" David said.

"Big shot," the girl said, and pulled a face.

"No one prefers walking to flying," I said.

"How'd he learn to walk, anyway?"

"We taught him."

"Perhaps you've crushed his spirit," she said.

"What do you mean?"

"Perhaps he's lost all emotional kinship."

"What?"

"With gulls. Perhaps he doesn't know he's a bird anymore."

"That's idiotic," Sandy said.

"Look at him squatting in the sand there," the girl said. "He probably thinks he's a crab."

"He knows *exactly* what he is," Sandy said. "He's a bird." She turned away from the girl in dismissal. Walking to the gull, she crouched beside him again and said, "You're a bird."

"Yes, missie," David piped.

"And birds fly."

"Yes, missie."

"And *you* are going to fly."

"Yes, missie."

"Now *fly!*" she shouted, and threw him into the air. He flew.

He soared up into the sky almost exultantly. The nylon line began to play out, uncoiling as the bird went higher and higher and finally wrenching up tight against the piece of driftwood.

"Now what?" I asked.

"Now we yank him down," Sandy said.

"Don't you dare!" the girl shouted. "You'll break his neck."

"We'll play him in gently," Sandy said, "like a kite," and she began easing the bird down, pulling in the line hand over hand, forcing him lower and lower until at last he spread his wings wide and flapped them in the now familiar braking motion, and dropped again to the sand.

"Good bird," Sandy said, and patted him on the head. "Give him some garbage, somebody."

I was in charge of the garbage detail. I reached into the oily bag and tossed the bird a moldy piece of orange. He swallowed it whole. It was easy to see how he had once managed to get a fishhook caught in his throat.

"Okay," Sandy said, "here we go again." She lifted

the bird, and, holding him tightly between both hands, swung him back and then forward again in a wide arc, releasing him suddenly.

The bird opened his wings.

He braked and fluttered down to the sand.

"You goddamn stupid bird," Sandy said.

"Let's go for a swim," David said.

"I don't know how to swim," the girl said.

"I wasn't asking you."

"Are you still here?" Sandy asked.

"Yes, I'm still here. I want to see what happens."

"He'll fly, that's what'll happen."

"Maybe he'll try it himself if we leave him alone," David suggested.

"What's the point of that?" Sandy said. "We want him to know we approve."

"You're only going to make him more neurotic than he is."

"Approval never made anyone neurotic," the girl said.

"Let's take a dip anyway," I said. "It's hot as hell."

"I don't know how to swim," the girl said again.

"How'd I ever get involved with such quitters?" Sandy said. But she came into the water with us.

The dark-haired girl sat on the shore and watched us swim for a while. When it became apparent we were going to ignore her, she got to her feet and walked down to the water's edge, testing it with her toes, glancing at us every now and then. At last, she wandered off up the beach, looking back at us only once before she climbed over the dune and disappeared.

"Good riddance," Sandy said.

When we came out of the water, we were all too tired to try with the bird again. We rolled up the line, put the leash back on his collar, and walked up the beach to Sandy's house. There was a note waiting for her on the kitchen table.

Sandy darling:
  I have gone into the city to meet Mr. Caudell for
dinner. There is food in the freezer. I will be
catching the early boat back tomorrow morning.
                                    Love,
                                    Mother


  "I've got a great idea," Sandy said. "Let's go over to
the mainland for chowder and lobster."
  "I don't think my folks would let me," David said.
"Not so soon after being grounded."
  "Give it a try."
  "Where's your phone?"
  He called his parents, and to his surprise they said it
would be all right. We both went home to change our
clothes, and then met Sandy on the dock in time to
catch the six o'clock ferry over.
  The dark-haired girl was sitting on one of the pil-
ings, watching us.


  We had lobster and chowder at a place called Lam-
bert's, and then we walked over to the movie house to
find out what was playing. The feature was scheduled
to start at 8:10 and break at 10:20, which meant we
could see the show and still catch the last ferry back to
Greensward at eleven o'clock. We stood on the sidewalk under the marquee and counted our money. A
few hulking townie kids were nudging each other over
near the glass cases where the movie posters were,
ogling Sandy's miniskirt and bare feet. We ignored
them completely. We had just enough money to pay
for our admission, but we had already bought round-
trip tickets on the ferry, so we decided to go in.
  The movie was exceptionally good.
  It was about man's alienation from his society, we
decided later on. It was also about the difference between illusion and reality. A sign at the box office
warned that the picture was recommended for mature

audiences, but nobody questioned our maturity, so we
didn't bring up the matter either. The film was made
by a French director and was set in the city of Los Angeles, California. The first shot was of a young man
surfing in at Malibu. He comes ashore onto this empty
beach where a girl surfer is waiting for him. They
begin making out like mad, and then the titles come
on, and the guy and the girl get into a red T-bird, and
he drops her off someplace and then continues driving
out through those brown California hills, the air all
shimmering around him, almost as if the hills themselves are a mirage, the photography was really quite
excellent.

It turns out that the young man is really an actor
working in a weekly television series. He makes a great
deal of money, and he's very efficient at what he does,
which is portraying the owner of a small nightclub in
Santa Monica. The weekly series was gone into in
great detail because it expressed the contemporary
confusion between illusion and reality. As the owner of
this nightclub, the hero becomes involved in the lives
of everyone who comes into the place, usually helping
them to resolve their problems before the hour is over.
The irony, of course, is that the man playing the hero
of the series is incapable of solving his own real-life
problems, whereas he is portraying a level-headed, sen-
sible person in the film within the film.

The television series, too, provides the opportunity
for some sex stuff, because naturally there's a chorus
line and some strange, disreputable LSD and surfing
types, all part of the film within the film, which shows
the actor at work as the hero in some very exciting
footage in the dressing room of one of the dancers.
Then the director calls "Cut," and we're left with the
impression that this love-making with the girl was all
make-believe. In fact, the actor's *life* in that studio out
in the Valley someplace is all make-believe, and we

begin to wonder where the reality lies, it was very interesting.

In order to make contact in this impersonal world
where his days are full of phony fistfights and love
scenes with the director calling "Cut," the actor be-
longs to a legitimate theater group at night, and he
goes there to try acting seriously. But even there (in
his real life now and not in the weekly television phony
life) he finds himself surrounded by people who are
more interested in the plays they're doing than their
own very real and personal problems. Also, in addition
to the hero's fake television work and his even phonier
nighttime acting, he's involved in some very suspicious
comings and goings to San Diego and the naval base
there—in short, he's a spy. This was not as far out as
it sounds because the spying was made to seem like an
extension of this man's estrangement, spying being a
job without a product, a detached sort of work in
which even the old slogans like patriotism and freedom
become lost in all the double-crossing done by both
sides, boy what a picture.

Then, at rehearsal of the theater group one night,
after the hero has taken detailed pictures of a nuclear
submarine in San Diego, something happens that
causes him to reconsider his entire way of life.

He finds a baby in his T-bird.

He goes inside to where everyone is rehearsing a
scene from *Who's Afraid of Virginia Woolf?* and he
asks if anyone left a baby in his car. Nobody seems to
know anything about the baby, and besides they're
more interested in exploring the intense reality of Martha and George. So he goes out to the car again and,
instead of calling the police (on the ferry ride home,
we tried to figure out why he didn't call the police—
probably because he was a spy), he takes the baby
home with him. This is the first time there's been anything real in his life, you see, an innocent baby, who
incidentally symbolizes hope for the new generation.

Well, to make a long story short, he doesn't know anything about child care, and when the baby gets sick one night, he fails to call the doctor in time because he's making out with two Chinese starlets in the bedroom upstairs, and the baby dies, which symbolizes the death of all hope for even the new generation, pretty grim. I know it sounds rather confusing in synopsis, but it was really crystal clear when you watched it.

The end of the film was a masterpiece. Even the New York critics said it wrapped up the entire story and gave added meaning and dimension to everything that had preceded it. You have to remember that the film was about illusion and reality and alienation, and you have to remember that everything in this man's life was false, except the spying. The spying was illusory and unreal, yes, but it was not false. That is to say, he was *really* taking pictures of submarines, and he was *really* passing these pictures on to the enemy, and he was *really* receiving money for this undercover activity, even though the money was nowhere near what he earned as a television actor. There was a sense throughout, right up to the end, of a basic truthfulness to this dirty work: however filthy and horrible and double-crossing it may have been, it was at least down to earth and honest. And then came the zinger, wow, it zipped in there like a lightning bolt, it actually sent chills up my spine. This man—now hold onto your hats—this man didn't even *know* he was a spy! That's right! He'd been brainwashed to *believe* his cover occupation, and he didn't have the faintest inkling that he was passing secrets to the enemy! Why, if you had tortured him and hung him by his thumbs he would not have been able to tell you he was a spy, because all he knew was that he was a television actor. So the point was triumphantly made that even in this very dirty business of spying, there was no involvement. In short, there was no involvement anywhere. That was the end of the picture, and it was a very exciting picture. Sandy let us feel her up all the way through it.

It started during the scene at the movie studio out in the Valley, where the actor who is a spy is portraying the nightclub owner and is in the dancer's dressing room, where she is wearing only a robe. Sandy was sitting between us, her right hand in David's, her left hand in mine. She suddenly gave a slight startled gasp and tightened her hand on mine. I thought she was responding to what was happening on the screen, because the actor portraying the nightclub owner was at that moment lowering the dancer's robe to her waist, her back to the audience, of course. I squeezed Sandy's hand and glanced at her and saw that she had turned to whisper something to David, who now shook his head. Sandy giggled. I looked back at the screen and was startled to discover that the actress playing the dancer had turned to face the camera with her breasts fully exposed. I wondered for a moment why an actress would allow this, and then I remembered that Sandy had done exactly the same thing for me in the forest, and then, suddenly, she squeezed my hand again and brought it swiftly to her breast.

On the screen, the actor and the dancer were kissing, he was brushing her hair away from her ear, his hand came up to fondle her breast, the camera showed him caressing her. Sandy clasped her hands in her lap, sitting very still, watching the screen, the dancer's lips parting, filling the screen now, the actor's mouth joining hers, and it was then that I realized David's hand was under her sweater. I dropped my own hand to her waist, remembering she had not allowed me to do this to her when we were alone together in the forest, found the bottom edge of her sweater, and eased my hand under it and up over her ribs to her bra. On the screen, the director yelled "Cut!" to illustrate the alienation. Sandy crossed her legs, and I looked down at the short skirt and wanted to put my hand on her thigh, but was afraid to. I glanced sidewards at David, hoping he would do it first. The actor walked off the set and took a Coke handed to him by one of the grips or somebody, and then went straight off the sound stage and out onto the studio lot where the sunshine was bright and cowboy extras smoked against the sides of buildings painted gray. A tall blond girl carrying a clipboard came out of one of the studio cottages and smiled at the actor, who waved at her as he got into his red T-bird. He looked up at the sky, a white California sky, squinting, and then revved the engine. Sandy uncrossed her legs, and leaned toward David, and then leaned back toward me. She did not look at either of us. Her eyes were on the motion picture screen.

The Santa Monica hills were brown, and roadside signs warned that this was a Fire Area. The hero drove through it with his eyes squinted, smoking a cigarette, squealing around every curve in the freeway. He drove up onto a wide avenue identified as Sunset Boulevard, continued driving onto Sunset Strip and then pulled into a hamburger joint where a redheaded carhop in a short skirt and boots came over to take his order. I looked at Sandy's legs again. I kept wishing that the hero of the movie would find another girl and undress her. He found another girl soon enough: there were girls sprinkled everywhere through the picture. When he pulled in for gas, in fact, I expected the station attendant to be a tall brunette in skin-tight slacks, but she wasn't. The next girl didn't appear until the hero went to his evening dramatics group someplace on Wilshire Boulevard, I believe it was, and she was an aspiring actress of about seventeen, just a little older than Sandy, with breasts very much like Sandy's when they were finally revealed in a scene outdoors under the eucalyptus trees where she and the actor wrestled playfully for a while until he stripped her down naked, she giggling all the while and Sandy's nipple growing hard. I began to feel terribly grubby about what we were doing because the theater was very brightly lighted for a little hick theater, and I was certain everyone knew exactly what was going on. Once, when my fingers brushed David's, I smiled and then idiotically thought I had laughed aloud, and quickly looked over my shoulder to make certain no one was watching us. The interesting thing about it all was that the people on the screen were actually doing much more than we were in our seats, which possibly was the point of the film, after all: our hang-up with illusion, our putdown of reality. In other words, was the play-acting on the screen more exciting than what was *really* going on with Sandy? I don't think I actually wondered that at the time, in fact I'm sure I didn't. I was too caught up in what was happening, you see, too thoroughly bombarded by images flashing in beautiful color sequence before my eyes, the two young starlets in the bedroom with the hero, the baby writhing in fever downstairs, Sandy's smooth brown legs crossing and recrossing, the now familiar feel of her breast, the awareness of my own immense masculinity, and the further knowledge of our secret, the secret we three shared, we could *do* this, she would allow us to *do* this.

On the way to the ferry slip, we talked about the film. The street bordering the bay was silent and dark. Most of the business district was built inland, of course, and as a result there never *was* too much action along the bay front. But this was still comparatively early on a Saturday night, and you didn't expect the sidewalks to be pulled in right after dinner. It was sort of eerie. Here we were in the midst of what was supposed to be civilization, but the only sign of life came from a fisherman's bar spilling orange and blue neon into the street up ahead.

"He wasn't involved with *any* of them," David said, "that was the point. None of the people in that picture ever really touched each other."

"There was something very phony about that picture," Sandy said. "I mean, if the point was that all that running around and fooling around was so unattractive, then why did the director make it so exciting?"

"That's exactly what *I* thought," I said.

"On the other hand," Sandy said, "maybe the excitement had nothing to do with the movie."

David and I said nothing. We both knew what she meant, but we were somewhat startled that she was willing to talk about it, even though we'd agreed to be completely honest with each other.

"Maybe it had to do with touching me," she said. "And getting me so hot I thought I would faint," she said, and that was when the three boys appeared on the sidewalk ahead of us. We had just passed the bar, and we were bathed in an eerie disharmony of vivid orange and blue, surprised by Sandy's frankness, more than a little unsettled by the sudden appearance of the trio ahead. They were standing in a loose-hipped imitation of every teenage hoodlum pose they had ever seen, the perfect stereotype of black leather-jacketed youth, except that they were wearing tee shirts and levis. The image was identical nonetheless, a trite reproduction of evil intent. And because we had been exposed to it so many times before, and recognized it immediately, our response was clichéd as well: immediate fear coupled with a pounding sense of imminent danger, a rising excitement at the prospect of a rumble. We turned without a word to each other and began running. The boat was supposed to leave for Greensward at eleven sharp. It was now close to 10:45, and we had no doubt that the boat was already in and loading passengers. It occurred to me, as we ran up the street away from the ferry slip, that we could very easily miss the boat and be trapped here on the mainland with three specimens who, it was fair to surmise, were not overly interested in discussing illu-

sion, reality, or alienation. I had no idea whether or
not they were the same boys who had been ogling
Sandy outside the theater before the picture began. But
there was an urgency in the clatter of their chase, and
I began to think we were making a mistake by running
deeper into a town they undoubtedly knew well, rather
than heading for the protection of the ferry waiting
room and the civilized people boarding the boat for
Greensward.

And then—I don't know what caused it, perhaps it
was the influence of the film, perhaps we were all still
deeply caught up in the film's message—a sudden gid-
diness came over the three of us. As we ran through
the deserted streets of the town, we began giggling, and
then laughing aloud. Behind us, one of the townies
yelled, "Hey, Long Legs, wait up!" and another one
shouted, "Give us a peek at you, honey!" and rather
than striking terror into our hearts, their words absolutely broke us up. The laughter was a curious thing in
that we recognized it might affect our ability to run,
and yet we couldn't stop it. I was developing a stitch in
my side, partly from running, partly from laughing,
and Sandy was gasping for breath as we rounded a
corner and cut across a vacant lot behind the drugstore. "Come on, Long Legs," one of the townies
shouted, "we ain't gonna hurt you," and David said,
"Not much," and we all burst out laughing again. "Get
rid of them two queers," one of the boys yelled, and I
said, "Hit him with your purse, David," all of this
while we were tearing across the lot and avoiding bottles and piles of ashes and bags of garbage and trying
to figure out a way to circle around back toward the
ferry slip, laughing wildly. They must have thought we
were crazy. Maybe we were. It seemed to me, though,
that the reality of the chase, even the reality of the
menace it represented, had been diminished by the fact
that we had lived it too often before, if only vicari-
ously. How real could these hoods behind us be when

they were shouting banalities like, "Come on, honey, we got something for you," or "Slow down, baby, you'll love it?" How real could any of this idiotic chase be when we had already witnessed wilder chases on motion picture screens? Laughing, stumbling, our eyes tearing, we came out onto a long dark street flanked on one side by a closed supermarket and on the other by a closed dry-cleaning store, a closed bookshop, and a closed Italian restaurant with a sign announcing the house specialty as veal parmigana. The misspelling on the sign caught my eye as we rushed past, commenting beyond any doubt on the quality of the house specialty and further adding another dimension of fantasy to the chase, an Italian restaurant that could not spell in Italian. Out of breath, David said, "Do we stand and fight?" and Sandy said, "Shit, no," which caused more laughter, while behind us the hoods were getting more and more agitated. And then, through luck or intuition, we made an abrupt right turn and found ourselves once again on the street with the open bar, its blue and orange neon flashing ahead like some gaudy oasis. "Let's go, gang!" David shouted, and we began running faster and in dead earnest, though still chuckling with recognition of the absurdity of it all. Behind us, the cleverest of the townies shouted, "Aw, baby, don't be mean," and Sandy shouted, "Goodnight, lover," as we saw the ferry slip ahead. The boat was already in. We boarded it rapidly just as the three hoods came panting onto the dock, standing again in stereotyped tough-guys-hands-on-hips postures while we mingled with the other passengers, and then tauntingly thumbed our noses at them from the quarterdeck. Sandy laughed then, a high blaring hoot that caused some of the other passengers to turn and stare at us, a derisive challenge to the gangsters below. Tossing her golden hair in the light of the pilot house, she looped her arms through ours and led us aft.

We stood on deck all the way out to the island. It

was a marvelous night, and we huddled close together and sang songs in very low voices, and once David interrupted to ask Sandy whether she had really almost fainted, and she nodded briefly and quietly and with an odd embarrassment, and we kissed either side of her face spontaneously.

The very next day, the gull flew over our heads without a tether.

The extraordinary thing about it was its simplicity.

It was no secret that I didn't exactly agree with Sandy about the gull's intelligence. It seemed to me, in fact, that any number of other birds could have been leash-trained more quickly than he was. And the experience of the day before, when Sandy had succeeded in getting him to fly once—but *only* once—seemed to back up my earlier findings: the bird was stupid.

Nevertheless, bright and early on the morning of July 23, which was a Sunday, the four of us marched out to the point again, and again wrapped the end of our fishline around the heavy piece of driftwood half-submerged in the sand. It was while we were fastening the other end of the line to the bird's collar that Sandy got her brilliant inspiration.

"Why do we need the line at all?" she asked.

Without waiting for an answer (we were, in truth, incapable of giving an answer, since this was only eight o'clock in the morning and we were both accustomed to sleeping a bit later that summer, especially on Sundays), she marched directly to the bird while he and we blinked stupidly and together, removed the collar from around his throat, and then backed away from him. David was the first of us to come to his senses.

"Goodby, gull," he said.

"Shhh," Sandy said, and signaled to us with her hand, the palm flat, patting the air. The gull peered up at us, unaware for the moment that the collar had been taken from his neck, completely oblivious to his freedom. We backed still further away from him, and he began following us up the beach, walking with that curiously proud gait of his, but never once attempting to fly.

"He is by far the stupidest bird in the world," I said.

"Shh," Sandy said again.

"Let's rush him," David said.

"No, just be quiet," Sandy said.

We squatted in the sand.

It was a gray day, heavy with mist that hovered over water and beach, a mist that would undoubtedly be burned off by midmorning. The sand was cool and damp. Far out on the water, a trawler made its slow way north toward Violet's island. There was a stillness to the point that morning, intensified by the hanging mist. The surf was gentle, washing in against the shore in endless whispering repetition, as tranquil as the water on the bay side. I thought of the film we had seen the night before, and I thought again about reality and illusion, and it seemed to me that even the flat ripples out there were only imitations of real waves. And then I thought about estrangement, not in the movie's sense, but instead as something you deliberately chose, an isolation you wanted and needed. And I thought, as I sat there between David and Sandy, that the three of us would go on this way forever, in a soft and misty landscape, understanding each other completely without having to say a word. Sitting on the edge of the shore, I was struck by a sense of eternity, the ocean stretching endlessly to distant places I had never seen, the mist wafting in to insulate and protect a very special universe, the nucleus of which was the three of us alone,

The bird suddenly took wing.

The beauty of his flight was breathtaking, it almost brought tears to my eyes. Wings flapping, he soared up into the mist, gray merging with gray, white underbelly and ruff looping upward, beak thrust into the sky. His wings—angled, long, graceful, tapered—went suddenly motionless. He swooped low in a descending arc, wings wide, and then flapped them again effortlessly, nudging himself higher and higher, until at last he was lost completely in the mist. We waited. The mist shifted soundlessly around us, the ocean whispered in against the shore.

"He's gone," David said.

"No, wait," Sandy said.

I don't know how long we waited. We stood almost shoulder to shoulder, gazing up at the sky, listening. The only sound was the incessant stroke of ocean against shore. And then, suddenly, the bird broke through the mist, his wings wide, emerging from the grayness as if a piece of it had suddenly broken away and was falling swiftly earthward, swooping lower and lower, more clearly defined now, the white startlingly explosive against the background of gray, the yellow of his beak and eyes, his legs tucked back against his body, closer and closer to the ground, the wings suddenly rising in eaglelike majesty to fan the air and brake his fall as he dropped silently to the sand at our feet.

"Feed him, quick," Sandy whispered.

David threw him a piece of bread. The bird gobbled it down at once.

"Now head up the beach. Fast! Run!"

We all began running, Sandy in the lead. She headed into the mist with long steady strides, was swallowed by it, disappeared into it, emerged again on a clear patch of beach, and was once again overwhelmed by the clinging tendrils of fog. I stopped and looked behind me. The gull was still sitting.

"Come on, bird!" I shouted, and on signal he ran several steps forward with his head thrust low, taking flight again and following us into the fog. Breathless, we clung together, waiting. He appeared above our heads at last, wings wide, circling, swooping, and then dropping to the beach at our feet. David immediately gave him an apple core.

"He knows," Sandy said.

We ran back and forth along the beach until we were exhausted. Each time the bird took off into the air and followed us, and then descended again, and waited for his reward. The real test came when he was joined by a flock of gulls that came in suddenly off the fog-swathed water, shrieking and cawing in anticipation of food. The bird joined the flock, swooping and diving and circling and darting, raising his voice with theirs, and then coming to rest on the beach when the other birds did. But when we fed none of them, they all took wing again, except our bird, who waited patiently until David pulled another scrap from the bag of garbage.

Sandy grinned and said, "He's trained." Walking to the bird, she reached out her hand to pat him on the head—and he bit her.

She yanked back her hand. A look of startled rage crossed her face. "You fucking idiot!" she shrieked, and reached for him again, lips skinned back, teeth bared as if to return the bite. Something slid into her eyes. Intelligence or guile, cunning or concern, it jarred her to an immediate stop. Trembling, she forced a smile onto her mouth and airily said, "It's only a scratch, men."

"Is the skin broken?" David asked.

"No."

"He was eating," I said, apologizing for the bird.

"He almost ate *me,*" Sandy said, and laughed. She turned to the gull. Without a trace of her earlier flaring anger, she cheerfully said, "Come on, bird."

We began walking up the beach. Behind us, the gull took flight. He followed us all the way to Sandy's house. When we went inside for lunch, he sat on the deck and waited for us.

The next day, he was gone.

Sandy related the disappearance to me on the telephone, and I immediately called for David and we walked together up the beach to Sandy's house, speculating on what might have happened. She had reported that the night before, unwilling to take any chances, she had once again put the leash on the bird and tethered him to the deck railing. This morning, when she'd gone outside to feed him, the leash was still attached to its stanchion, but the gull had somehow managed to escape by squeezing his neck and his head through the collar. I thought this was an amazing stunt for such a stupid bird, but David said I wasn't considering the fact that the bird had once tasted freedom and probably couldn't bear even temporary bondage any longer. He then told the story of a chain-gang convict who'd freed himself from his manacles by chopping off his right hand. He'd died fifteen feet from where his severed hand lay in the dust, but at least he'd died free. I immediately conjured a vision of a decapitated gull taking wing from Sandy's porch, only to crash into the nearby bushes, his head and neck still circled by the collar fastened to the leash and the railing. When we got to her house, Sandy seemed calm enough, considering she'd lost the bird after all the time and energy put into his training. We sat around disconsolately for a while, trying to figure out what to do, and finally decided to conduct an extensive search.

We looked everywhere for that damn bird.

We started in the bushes nearest the house because I was still entertaining the notion of a headless bird crash-diving immediately after takeoff, but the gull was nowhere in the vicinity, nor were there any traces of feathers anywhere. We lengthened our radius, swinging out from the house in a widening circle that took us onto the beach at one end and close to the forest on the other. Sandy gave up the search before either David or I were weary. Determined to find the bird and surprise her, we continued looking long into the afternoon, luring flocks of gulls down to the beach with our bag of garbage, hoping to recognize our bird among them.

By sunset, we were on the edge of the forest.

"Do you think he may have wandered in there?" David asked.

"I doubt it."

"Let's try it."

"I don't think he's in there," I said. I was suddenly afraid of the forest again. I knew it was harmless, but something urged me not to enter it, something warned me that whatever horrors it had earlier contained were still in there, ready now to spring full-blown from nightmare into reality.

"Come on," David said, and began walking toward the black and twisted pines.

The sun was low on the horizon, orange, silhouetting the charred trees, recreating that night so long ago when flames had leapt from branch to branch and the islanders had trembled in fright on the distant shore. The sun drove fire directly into the eye, overpowering the retina, blinding unless a gnarled limb or twisted trunk intercepted its rays, shooting sparks from behind black contorted trees, now and again blocked by large gray boulders that cast long shadows on the forest floor, translating, by collision, pure light into something as dark and as deep as an open grave. There were nameless horrors in this forest, I felt them ooze damp and white from every pore of my body, heard them shriek inside my head with all the crackling terror of a flying spark, saw them materialize in bursting sunfans, a woman in white nylon, her face melting. There was no wind. I followed close behind David, longing for a reassuring word from him. But he was as silent as the forest around us, and I suspected he was as frightened as I.

The black boulder lay just ahead. I recognized it instantly as the one behind which Sandy and I had sat the day we filled out the computer questionnaire. Huge and round, it rose from among the smaller gray rocks like an ancient crypt.

The bird was lying behind the boulder.

He was still wearing the red collar and leash. There was red everywhere. Red in his white wing feathers and ruff, red on his broken yellow beak and crushed skull, red splattered onto the black boulder, red on the forest floor, red that shrieked against the violent orange of the dying sun, the forest was red, the world was red with the blood of the gull.

A rock rested on the ground some three feet from his body. It was covered with his drying blood. We looked at the gull, and we looked at the rock that had been used to crush his skull, and a slow comprehension came to us, but without horror. It was as though, expecting the worst from this place, we were now unafraid of anything less than the worst. And then, I don't know why, we were both suddenly overcome with rage.

"You dumb bird!" David said, and picked up the blood-stained rock. I had moved simultaneously, and of my own volition, to pick up the nearest weapon at hand, a rock larger than the one David wielded. We threw the rocks as though on signal, and then we gathered more rocks, hurling them at the bird in rising frenzy, rock after rock, finally exhausting the supply at our feet and, sobbing now, seized fallen limbs which we used to club and batter and pound until the bird lay pulverized, a sodden mass of feathers and gristle and pulp.

We stood over him in tears, exhausted. Our hands and our clothes were covered with blood.

As we walked out of the forest, it occurred to me that we had never even given the stupid gull a name.

# TWO:

## *RHODA*

SANDY'S MOTHER GAVE A HUGE COCKTAIL PARTY ON the last Sunday in July.

The alleged purpose of the party was to bid farewell to those islanders who had rented for only half the summer, but Sandy's mother was a person who seized upon *any* excuse for a party, and probably would have thrown one anyway, if just to herald the coming of the regatta the following Wednesday.

David and I were at the party, which started at three P.M., only because Sandy's mother had come to the island without help, and Sandy had offered our services free of charge for the afternoon. Her mother didn't relish the idea at first, primarily because she had read about Greenwich, Connecticut, kids getting drunk at adult parties and causing automobile accidents and scandals, but we assured her we would participate only as waiters, refilling empty glasses, serving *hors d'ouevres,* and generally helping to ease the flow of traffic in and around the house. Since she had invited sixty-four people (certain disaster if it rained), and since her staff, before our generous offer, was to consist only of Mr. Caudell (the Pine Street lawyer) and her daughter, she eventually came around to seeing things our way, provided we "didn't get underfoot."

The day was sunny and clear.

Mr. Caudell had arrived on Friday night to spend the weekend. Sandy's mother, with commendable propriety, always put up a cot for him in the living room, though it was Sandy's observation that the bedclothes never seemed rumpled in the morning and many a

87

floorboard squeaked at night in the passageway between the living room and her mother's bedroom. He greeted David and me on the rear deck, where he had set up his bar. He was wearing a sports shirt with a loud Hawaiian print, over which he had put on a red bar apron decorated with the legend "Don't Kiss Me, I'm Cooking." Neither David nor I understood the apron's connection with Mr. Caudell's bartending duties, but we made no comment.

"It's a gorgeous day, isn't it?" Mr. Caudell said.

"Wonderful," David said. "Is there anything we can do before the guests arrive?"

"Just relax, plenty to do later on," Mr. Caudell said. "I'm certainly glad I'm not on the beach today. I turn lobster red in the sun."

Sandy came out of the house just then and said, "Oh, hi, I didn't hear you."

"Hi," I said.

"Hi," David said.

She was wearing big golden hoop earrings and a blue shift. Even barefoot, she was taller than Mr. Caudell, who came up to about her left ear. David and I were wearing clean chinos, sneakers, and our blue Mr. Porter shirts. The three of us looked very good.

"Whatever happened to that bird you were training?" Mr. Caudell asked.

"His head hit a rock and he was killed," Sandy answered immediately, and then glanced at us. The glance was significant.

Last Monday night, after we'd discovered the dead gull in the forest, David and I had first gone home to wash and change our clothes. (David's mother, of course, asked him where he had got all that blood on him. After the incident with the beer, she was convinced that her son was a psychopathic criminal, and I'm sure she assumed he had murdered some innocent old man on the dock. He told her we'd been fishing and had cleaned our catch afterward, hence the blood

and gore. She bought it.) We had then gone over to
Sandy's house and asked her to take a walk with us on
the beach. Huddled over a small wood fire David built
in the sand, we told her it was our understanding that
there were to be no secrets between us. (Yes, she said,
that's right, that's certainly true.) Well, we said, not
only had she kept a secret, but she had actually lied to
us. (No, Sandy said, how can you even *think* such a
thing?) We can think such a thing, we said, because
she had told us the bird had slipped his leash and
flown away, when it was plainly apparent to both of us
that she had led him into the forest and bashed in his
skull.

The wood fire crackled and sputtered into the long
silence. The waves pounded in against the shore.

"Why did you kill him?" David asked.

"I don't know," Sandy said.

"You *must* know," I insisted.

"He was a stupid bird," she said, and suddenly burst
into tears. I watched her twisted face in the light of the
fire, remembering our own anger, our own bitter tears
after we had pounded the gull beyond recognition.

"I'll never lie to you again," Sandy said, and that,
after all, was the most important thing about the entire
incident, this strengthening of the bond between us.

Her glance now was secretive and assuring. She was
answering Mr. Caudell's question honestly, lying to
*him* of course, but once again affirming *our* unity.

"That's a shame," Mr. Caudell said. "Point of fact,
he was a most intelligent bird."

I was spared answering him by the timely arrival of
The Dynamiters, an island rock-and-roll group hired
for the party by Sandy's mother. The leader of the
group was a kid named Dexter, whom everyone called
Deuce, and who resembled a large sheepdog with
glasses. He played lead guitar and sang. The rhythm
guitarist was a kid who tried to hide his acne by keeping his head ducked at all times. His name was Phil,

and he was a very bad musician who sang backup in a high whiny nasal voice. A kid named Arthur, whose father was a doctor, played bass guitar, and the drummer (the only good musician in the bunch) was a year-round islander whose family owned the plumbing supply store over near Mr. Porter's. His name was Danny. The Dynamiters were all about thirteen, short and somewhat scrawny-looking, and they arrived with four thousand dollars worth of electronic equipment, including amplifiers and microphones enough to broadcast a signal to Tokyo. Deuce, the leader of the group, shy in the presence of anyone, but especially girls, approached Sandy deferentially and said, "Excuse me, Miss, but where did you want us to set up?"

"I'll ask my mother," Sandy said, and went inside.

"Well, so you fellows are the band, huh?" Mr. Caudell observed brilliantly,

"Yessir," Deuce answered.

"What do you call yourselves?"

"The Dynamiters."

"I hope you don't have short fuses," Mr. Caudell said, and winked at David and me, and then burst out laughing.

"Nossir," Deuce answered, not getting the joke.

"What instrument do you play, son?" Mr. Caudell asked.

"Lead guitar, sir," Deuce said.

"Would you care for a soda or something?"

"Not right now, sir, thank you," Deuce said, and then smiled at me timidly and said, "Hi, Peter."

"Hi, Deuce."

"Hi, David."

"Deuce."

"Great day, huh?" Deuce said.

"Yeah," David said.

"Think we'll be setting up out here on the deck?"

"I doubt it," I said. "She'll probably put you down there on the lawn."

"Gee, I hope our extension cords reach," Deuce said.

Sandy came out of the house again and said, "Mother wants you down on the lawn."

"Gee, I hope our extension cords reach," Deuce said again, and went down to tell the other boys in the group. They held a brief consultation at the bottom of the porch steps. One of the boys—it was difficult to tell which one because they were in a huddle—said in a high squeaky voice, "Well, why the hell can't we play on the deck there?" and Deuce answered, "Because she wants us here on the lawn," and another boy said, "I mean, man, they won't even be able to *hear* us down here."

"You fellows want a soda or something?" Mr. Caudell asked us.

"No, thank you," David said.

"Hey, you look handsome," Sandy said to me.

"Thanks."

"You, too," she told David.

"Here come the first guests," he answered, and pulled a face.

The first guests were Violet, in a green muu muu, and Frankie and Stuart, the two fags who ran The Captain's, down near the old ferry slip. The Captain's was a shack overlooking the bay, and it had got its name because Frankie had decorated it with nets and anchors and lobster pots and buoys and all things nautical in an attempt to disguise the undisguisable fact that it was a shack. Neither Frankie nor Stuart were obnoxious fruits, meaning they didn't go mincing around or making sexy little jokes about *Oh, you're such a cute one, I'd love to give you such a pinch*, the way some faggots do, especially the ones in the city along Greenwich Avenue. Frankie had been living with Stuart for half his life, almost as though they were married. Stuart had a black handlebar mustache, and he never said very much. Frankie was blond, and he made up for Stuart's reticence, talking almost nonstop in a high grating voice. They were both wearing Bermuda shorts and Italian sports shirts. Stuart also wore a wedding band.

"Hello, boys," Violet said to us, "what a surprise! Hello, David," she said, beaming, and David smiled and nodded, and then went inside to see if Sandy's mother needed any help in the kitchen. I introduced Mr. Caudell to Violet and the others, and then drifted down to the lawn while he mixed drinks for them. Sandy's mother heard voices and came out of the house. I was talking to Deuce when Sandy tiptoed up behind me and said, "Hi, handsome."

"Hi, gorgeous."

"You supervising the band?"

"Yep, getting everything organized down here, yep," I said, and nodded. "You know 'Paint It Black,' Deuce?"

"Sure," he said. "But that's like from the days of the chariot races, man."

"You know your fly is open?" Sandy whispered to me.

"No, but if you hum a few bars, I'll fake it," I said, and we both burst out laughing.

"What's so funny?" Phil asked, his head ducked to hide his acne.

"Private joke," Sandy told him.

"Give me an E," Arthur said to Deuce. Behind them, the drummer began a series of rolls designed to cause sections of the beach to break off and slide into the ocean.

"Not so *loud*," Sandy's mother called from the deck. "Peter, tell them not to play so loud."

"You heard her," I said.

"Loud? We're not even plugged *in* yet," Deuce complained.

"Sandy," her mother called, "may I see you a moment, please?"

Sandy went into the house and came out a few minutes later with a tray of canapés. I helped the Dynamiters lay out their extension cords across the lawn and into the house, where I found an outlet behind Mr. Caudell's unslept-in cot. Then I retraced the whole process because the cord was trailing across the entrance door and I was afraid somebody would break his neck going in or out. What I finally did was unhook the living-room screen at the bottom, and pull the cords in through the window. One of Mr. Caudell's old cigar butts was on the windowsill. David came out of the kitchen carrying a tray of glasses while I was plugging in the cords.

"The Dynamiters all set?" he asked.

"Yep."

"Looks like we're in for a musical treat," he said.

"Oh yes indeed," I said.

"How'd you like old Short Fuse?"

"Uncommonly hilarious," I said.

"I never thought he was humorous until today," David said. "Shows how wrong you can be about a fellow."

"Oh yes indeed," I said.

"Where's Sandy?"

"Out serving."

"I'd better bring these glasses out."

We went out together. The deck was fairly crowded now, and more people were coming up the boardwalk toward the house. I kept circulating among the guests, asking them if I might refill their glasses, and then asking them what they were drinking, and then carrying the empty glasses over to Mr. Caudell, who tended bar almost as excellently as he told humorous stories, point of fact. There wasn't much to do in the beginning, but by four o'clock, when almost everyone had arrived, Sandy and David and I got fairly busy. Mr. Matthews, the island councilman, was there of course, an honored guest whom no one dared call Tom except his wife.

(She, in fact, called him Tommy.) Everyone else called him Mr. Matthews, and they endowed the term of address with all the respect due the president of the United States. "Excuse me, Mr. Matthews, but we were wondering what your thoughts were on the proposed bridge to the island," or, "Excuse me, Mr. Matthews, but I'd like you to meet my sister-in-law, who's visiting for the weekend," or, "Excuse me, Mr. Matthews, but did you personally arrange this wonderful sunshine?" Mr. Matthews, meanwhile, could not take his eyes off Sandy, and along about 4:15 he maneuvered her into a corner of the deck and began telling her about his deep-sea fishing exploits the day before (apparently he was a big fisherman, too) while simultaneously trying to cop a feel under the protective cover of the canapé tray. I went over at that point and asked him if he would care for another drink, and then I told Sandy that Mr. and Mrs. Friedman over on the other side of the deck were saying they would like some more shrimp, so she escaped him and blew a kiss at me as she went by, and I brought his glass to Mr. Caudell and said, "Bourbon and water, very heavy on the bourbon," figuring the sooner we got the old bastard drunk and incapacitated, the sooner Sandy could relax.

David's parents weren't at the party because they had left the island the day before to attend a wedding in New Jersey. My parents, however, had arrived at about a quarter to four, and they kept calling me over to introduce me to this or that person, always seeming to take great pride whenever anyone said, "My, how *big* he is! Did you say he's only sixteen?" (to which my father invariably replied, "Sixteen going on twenty-four"). Actually, I was not, and *am* not, a tall person for my age, and I was surprised each time my parents were taken in by such flattery, nor could I figure out why they seemed so thrilled to hear I was *big*. I performed as expected, though, smiling shyly, and sir-ring everyone to death, and then offering to serve up some more *hors d'oeuvres* or carry off a glass that needed replenishing. My father's glass needed replenishing more than most people's, but that's because he's a connoisseur of good scotch, as he is terribly fond of saying. One night, after having connoisseured a great deal of good scotch, my father came into the bedroom where I was fast asleep. I was ten years old at the time. He woke me up, and then sat by the side of the bed and began crying.

"Oh, Peter," he kept saying, over and over again. "Oh, Peter."

I felt very strange that night. As if *I* was the father and *he* was the child. Very strange. Just "Oh, Peter," over and over again.

Every time my father asked for another scotch that afternoon of the cocktail party, my mother threw him a little warning dagger, green eyes snapping off the knife with a quick flick, *whap!*, right between the shoulder blades. But my father always smiled back at her in a gracious and loving and absolutely sober-seeming way, his gray eyes crinkling and assuring her he would know when he'd had too much, which he rarely knew until he was falling-down drunk and telling people once again that he was a connoisseur of good scotch. Everyone agreed that my father was just the most darling sweetest man in the whole world when he got drunk—except my mother. She called him a drunken pissing fool one night three summers ago while I was lying in my bed, without benefit of cuddly toy this time, being all of fourteen. That was the first inkling I had that perhaps my father drank a trifle too much at parties. The second inkling was in the city, when he drove the maid home after a party and nearly killed himself and her by ramming his Porsche into a lamppost. Everyone in the building knew that he had been drunk. I told the kids at school they were all crazy. That was when I was fifteen.

Last summer I was sixteen and serving drinks to guests at Sandy's mother's cocktail party, and trying very hard to keep my father from having one too many, which usually meant forty-four too many. I asked David to help keep the sauce away from him, but of course my father was a grown man capable of finding the bar all by himself, which he did with increasing regularity as the afternoon wore on. The Dynamiters, over constant threats of castration by Sandy's mother, turned up their amplifiers full-blast and nearly blew everyone off the deck, for nothing had they been named so colorfully. Violet began dancing a fat lady's version of the Frug, and most of the guests joined in, though hardly any of them knew what they were doing. The new dances are all on the upbeat, you see, and most people who learned to dance when my parents did are used to the downbeat, which is the one-and-three beat dominant in the Lindy and all of the other fast dances going all the way back to the Big Apple and the Shag and the Black Bottom, I guess. The Frug and the Monkey and the Watusi and all the other new ones, though, have the stress on the two-and-four beats, and it's very difficult to explain that to people who were raised with the beat of another generation in their heads. So whereas some of them were very good dancers (Frankie, for example, had an excellent sense of rhythm and style as he danced with Violet, snapping his fingers and tossing his blond locks), they simply weren't *with* the new beat; something looked wrong, distorted, *off*. I kept waiting for someone to say, "Let the kids do it; come on, kids, show us how to do it," but they had the good grace not to. Besides, the three of us were very busy by that time, plying our way to and from the bar, coming out of the kitchen with hot little cheese patties, and chestnuts wrapped in bacon, and frankfurters with sharp delicatessen mustard, and beautiful tiny shrimp, and toasted little tortillas fresh from the oven, feeding the horde of hungry guests, most of whom seemed to have arrived expecting dinner, even though the invitations (which David and I had helped Sandy and her mother address and mail) had clearly stated Cocktails 3:00–7:00.

Mr. Caudell used a very heavy hand on the booze bottle, and a lot of the guests were beginning to get that six o'clock glassy-eyed look, including Sandy's mother, who laughed too loud habitually, even when she wasn't high, and whose laugh, I now realized, Sandy had imitated on the ferry ride home that night the townies tried to rape her. (We really didn't know whether rape had been their intention, but we constantly referred to that night among ourselves as The Big Rape Scene.) It was Sandy who kept the flow of food coming from the kitchen, and a good thing too, because otherwise all those swilling islanders would have floated out to England on a sea of alcohol. When the sun finally went down, everyone turned to face the ocean, as though paying obeisance to a familiar deity. There were the usual "oooohs" and "ahhhhs" accompanying the sunset, the unvaried reaction that came every night of the summer, as though each successive sunset were a new and exciting experience instead of an identical replay of the one that had taken place the night before. The Dynamiters played right through the scintillating display out there on the horizon, blasting the deck and the house and the island itself with their own rendition of "Gloria," Deuce wailing the words and Phil feebly bolstering him. The drummer was a good musician but a loud one, and the other members of the group kept turning up their amplifiers louder and louder in an attempt to drown him out, all in vain. As the music got louder and louder, as Mr. Caudell's drinks got stronger and stronger, as the sky and the ocean and the beach and the deck got darker and darker, the guests got noisier and noisier, so that there was a cacophony of sound hanging on the night air, canopied by the distant silent stars and a full moon that brought, for an instant only, renewed sighs of "ahhhhh" and "oooooh." The conversation was deafening, it bounced from the deck, it reverberated against the rear wall of the house, it threatened to obliterate even The Dynamiters' detonations. "Sandra, you're a nice little girl," Mr. Matthews said, and put his arm around her and squeezed her. "Oh, *thank* you, Mr. Matthews," Sandy said, "but I must see if anything's burning in the kitchen." Frankie said, "Yes, but the terrible truth of Pinter's plays is exactly what makes them so excruciatingly human," to which Mrs. Collins said, "But I think his people are horrible," to which Stuart in one of his rare contributions said, *"All* people are horrible, darling."

"I adore these two boys," Violet said, putting her fat arms around Frankie and Stuart. "I just *adore* them. We have no secrets from each other, do we, boys?" and Frankie said, "Not a secret in the world," and Stuart merely nodded, looking pleased and embarrassed. Mr. Ogilvy, who was an editor at a publishing house said, "Yes, but try to understand the Negro's viewpoint. If he is forced to become an expatriate in order to become a man, why *should* he cling to any fond memories of this country?" Agnes Bergman, who was a close friend of Sandy's mother, said, "I'm sick of everybody always talking about the Negro. How about the white man, huh, how about him?" to which Mr. Ogilvy said, "You'd better get used to people talking about the Negro," to which Agnes Bergman said, "Screw the Negro. I don't have to get used to anything I don't want to get used to," and David asked her if she would like another drink.

Mr. Patterson, who was a television executive, said, "Yes, but why do you think kids today are experimenting with all this crap?" and Mrs. Anhelm, who ran a notions shop in Queens, asked, "Why?" Mr. Patterson, grateful for the cue, nodded and said, "I'll tell you why," and Mr. Mannheim, who taught speech and dramatics at Columbia University, said, "I deal with youngsters every day of the week." Mr. Patterson said, "It's rebellion," and Mrs. Anhelm said, "It's their sex drive, that's what it is," and a woman wearing high-heeled shoes and a black bikini over which she had thrown a lacy robe that looked like a peignoir, said, "I'm from St. Louis." Mr. Patterson said, "They simply refuse to accept adult responsibilities." Mr. Mannheim said, "You'd be surprised how many of them are smoking pot," and Mrs. Anhelm said, "I once smoked Mary Jane at a party," and the woman in the black bikini said, "It's the Gateway to the West," and Mr. Mannheim said, "Did it turn you on?" and Mrs. Anhelm said, "I only smoked half a joint," and Mr. Patterson said, "They refuse to emulate," and Mr. Mannheim said, "It isn't hep to call it Mary Jane any more," and the woman in the black bikini said, "Hip."

"It isn't quite your proper bag," Deuce sang into the microphone, "the scene ain't yours, it's ours."

"Yes, but if we possess the power to blast them to hell and gone," Mr. Porter said, "then why don't we use it? Why are we holding back?"

"It's girl and boy," Deuce sang.

"Let's demolish them," Mr. Porter said, "annihilate them!"

"And flower joy," Deuce sang.

The man with Mr. Porter, his bald head peeling, his face as lobster red as Mr. Caudell claimed *his* got in the sun, said, "I agree of course," and Mr. Porter said, "Do you agree?" and the bald man said, "Of course, but what about retaliation?" Mr. Porter considered this for a moment, and then said, *"Let* them retaliate! It's a question of lasting power, that's all. We'll still be going strong after they're all dead and gone, *let* the bastards retaliate. Do you agree with me?" The bald man said, "Of course, I agree with you," and Mr. Porter said, "You agree with me, don't you?" and the bald man said, "Of course."

"It isn't quite your proper bag," Deuce sang, "the scene ain't yours, it's ours."

I took their empty glasses and carried them to the bar.

"Hello there, Sammy," Mr. Caudell said.

"It's Peter," I told him.

"Peter, Peter, pumpkin eater," he said, and laughed. "What'll it be, Peter, Peter, pumpkin eater?"

"Two scotches and soda," I said.

"Coming up. You want a little snort yourself, Peter, Peter pumpkin eater?"

"Thank you, I don't drink."

"Ho-ho, zat ees rich," Mr. Caudell said.

"It's true, though."

"What *do* you do, Peter, Peter, pumpkin eater?"

"I don't get you."

"With Sandy," he said, and winked.

"Why won't you let us set it right?" Deuce sang.

"I still don't get you," I said.

"Love all day and love all night . . ."

"Forget it, pal," Mr. Caudell said, and winked again, and mixed the drinks.

"Lulu had a baby," someone sang over Deuce's voice, "his name was Sonny Jim . . ."

"She put him in a pisspot . . ."

"Shhh, shhh, *die Kinder,*" someone said.

"It isn't quite your proper bag . . ."

"Two scotches and soda," Mr. Caudell said.

"The scene ain't yours, it's ours."

I picked up the glasses and carried them to where Mr. Porter and the bald-headed man were still talking.

"Because Goldwater himself advocated defoliation," Mr. Porter said, "don't you remember that?" the bald man said, "Of course I remember it," and Mr. Porter said, "You remember it, don't you?" and the bald man said, "Of course." Behind me, I heard my father telling someone, "I'm a connoisseur of good scotch," and then he grabbed me as I handed Mr. Porter his drink, and swung me around, and put his arm around my shoulders and said, "C'mere, Peter, tell these good people, am I a connoisseur of good scotch, or am I a connoisseur of good scotch?" I looked him in the eye, and I said, "You are a connoisseur of good scotch, Dad," and he said, "You bet your sweet ass I am." I excused myself just as someone said, "Is that your son? How old is he?" Behind me, I could hear my father saying, "Sixteen going on twenty-four," and then a woman laughed, and said, "He's so *big* for his age." Sandy was leaning over the deck railing, looking back over her shoulder as I approached.

"Hi," she said.

"Hi. Where's David?"

"Down with the band. He's making a request."

"What's he requesting? 'Far Far Away'?"

"Yok yok," Sandy said.

The amplifiers exploded into sound again with "Chelsea Bird," a hit expertly recorded by an English group and excruciatingly imitated now by Deuce and The Dynamiters. "Chelsea Bird, so cool, so nice, so cool like ice, so nice, so nice . . ."

". . . because in this day and age, there are only hypocrites and Puritans and nothing in between. I ask you, does . . ."

". . . Johnson really know what the fuck he's doing . . ."

"All the world dig her, all the world love her, Bristol, Taunton, Leeds, and London!"

". . . or is he only concerned about his precious image?"

"Blackburn, Bangor . . ."

". . . into a drugstore and says he wants to buy a deodorant, and the clerk says, 'Yes, sir, did you wish the roll-on ball type?' . . ."

*"Die Kinder . . ."*

". . . all the world dig her, all the world love her, Bangor, Blackburn, Leeds, and London!"

". . . 'No, thank you, just the regular underarm kind . . .' "

". . . of fools do they take the American public for?"

"Chelsea bird, so cool, so nice, so cool like ice, so nice, so nice . . ."

". . . I love them both, they're my precious sweethearts, these two darling boys."

"All the world dig her, all the world dig her, all the world dig her, mmm."

The voice suddenly cut through the cooperative din of the Dynamiters and the party guests, amplified and blaring from the group's expensive loudspeaker setup, overwhelming all other noise by sheer volume and ineptitude. Sandy and I both turned to look over the deck at the same moment, trying to pinpoint this new source of sound, this intrusive and cacophanous groan from below. An amber rectangle cast from the living-room window above illuminated three quarters of The Dynamiters plus a short, chunky, dark-haired girl who had commandeered Deuce's microphone and was holding it just below the head, as though producing, by her strangling grip on its neck, the horrible sound that permeated the night. We might not have recognized the girl as our friend from the beach had she not smiled in that moment, revealing her beautiful metal bands in what was doubtless intended to be a sexy grin accompanying the "Portsmouth, Dartmouth, Falmouth" line of the song. She continued slaughtering the lyrics as Deuce winced behind her, his head going deeper into his shoulders with each offkey bleat. Behind him, Phil's fear of acne exposure fled before an overwhelming curiosity as he lifted his face to see who was being sick on the lawn. David came rushing up the steps to the deck, laughing helplessly, running over to where Sandy and I stood with our mouths open, listening. The dark-haired girl would not relent. The lyrics resisted her, the amplifier feedback squeaked, the drummer tried to drown her out by playing even louder (a feat I would have thought impossible), and Deuce and the embarrassed Phil tried to recover their cool by singing stronger than she, but only succeeded in sounding out of tune against her flat and penetrating whine, "All the world dig her, all the world love her, Chelsea bird, mmm, Chelsea bird, mmm, Chelsea bird, mmm, dig her, dig," and the song ended.

The guests stood in drunken stupor and neurasthenic shock on the silent deck.

"Thank you very much," the dark-haired girl said into the microphone. "My name is Rhoda."

We took a walk along the beach after the party broke up.

There were a lot of parties on Greensward that night, and snatches of music drifted over the dunes, overlapping, and then getting lost in the steady murmur of the ocean. The moon had risen high and silvery over the water, dripping molten filigree from horizon to shore, illuminating the beach with a flat white light. The evening was soft, the distant stars blinked against a deep black void. We walked barefoot on the cold wet sand. We had already laughed ourselves silly over Rhoda and The Dynamiters, and now we were curiously silent, ambling up the beach without any clear destination in mind, stopping once to watch an airliner blink its red and green wing lights as it soared overhead, stopping again to listen to the clanging of a buoy far out on the water, and then picking up our steady gait again, the ocean on our left, the dunes dark with beach grass that rattled and whispered with each gentle gust of wind that came in off the water.

And then we sat on the edge of the shore; Sandy with her knees folded against her breasts, arms wrapped around them, skirts tucked in; David and I leaned back on locked elbows, legs stretched to where the water just touched our toes.

The night was so still.

The party sounds dissipated and then vanished completely, save for an occasional distant voice raised in farewell. There was a lingering sadness on the air, the knowledge that August was almost here, summer would soon be over. And then, as though giving voice to the permeating sense of grief, there was a sobbing sound behind us. Startled, we turned to look toward the dune, and saw nothing but the tall beach grass shifting in the ocean wind, illuminated by the brilliant moon. Puzzled, we looked at each other, and then Sandy got to her feet and walked swiftly to the dune. Climbing it, she signaled to us.

Rhoda was sitting with her face buried in her hands, sobbing bitterly.

"Who is it?" David said.

"It's Rhoda," I said.

"Go away," Rhoda said. She would not take her hands from her face. Her shoulders were heaving. She had stopped sobbing only long enough to utter her command and take in a fresh gulp of air.

"Come on, leave her alone," David said.

"No, wait a minute," Sandy said.

"Go away," Rhoda said again.

"She doesn't want us here, for Christ's sake, let's . . ."

"Can't you see she's crying?" Sandy said.

"Well, what's that got to do with anything?"

"He's right," I said. "Come on, Sandy."

"No," Sandy said.

"I can't stand crybabies," David said.

"Neither can I."

"Well then, go," Sandy said. "If you want to go, go." She sat beside Rhoda in the sand and put her arm around her. "What's the matter?" she said.

"Go away."

Rhoda was gasping for breath now, still sobbing and trembling. She turned away from Sandy and flung herself full length onto the sand, her face hidden in the crook of her elbow. Sandy touched her hair and said, "Rhoda?"

"Leave me alone."

"Come on, the hell with her," David said.

"Oh, shut up," Sandy said. "Can't you see she needs help?"

"I don't need help," Rhoda said, gasping.

"Now you just stop that crying," Sandy said. "Do you want to choke to death?"

"Nobody ever choked from crying," I said.

"If she wants to cry, let her cry," David said. "It's better than her singing, anyway," and Rhoda burst into fresh tears.

"Oh, Jesus Christ, listen to that," I said.

"Don't curse," Rhoda said, sobbing.

"Come on, get up," Sandy said.

"No."

"Get up, or I'll pick you up," Sandy said.

"Leave me alone."

"Leave her alone," David said, "she's a creep."

*"You're* a creep," Rhoda said, gasping and choking and rolling further away from Sandy, who seized her left hand, and yanked on it, getting her at last to a sitting position, and then putting one arm around her waist, and pulling her to her feet. Rhoda staggered about blindly, her eyes closed, shaking her head and hiding her face, trying to pull away from Sandy, who finally slapped her sharply, twice. The sobbing stopped at once. Gasping for breath, Rhoda stared fixedly at Sandy, tears streaming down her cheeks.

"You hit me," she said.

"You're damn right I did," Sandy answered.

"Now she'll go screaming to her mother," David said.

"My mother is dead," Rhoda said.

"Her mother is dead, you jackass," Sandy said.

Rhoda was making short brave snuffling sounds

now, as though wanting to break into tears again, but
afraid Sandy would hit her if she did. "Do you have a
handkerchief?" she asked.

"David?"

"*My* handkerchief?" David said, outraged.

"Oh, come *on,*" Sandy said.

"No," David said. "Absolutely not."

"She can have mine," I said, and reached into my
back pocket. "I haven't got one," I said.

"All right, damn it," David said, "here's mine." He
handed it to Rhoda and said, "Try not to gook it all
up, will you?"

"Thank you," Rhoda said, and noisily blew her
nose.

"How do you feel?" Sandy said.

"Terrible."

"Why?"

"They all laughed at me."

"That's because you're a lousy singer," David said.
Rhoda stopped in the middle of blowing her nose, and
gave him an injured look. I thought surely she would
begin crying again.

"You *are* a lousy singer," Sandy said.

"I'm better than Deuce."

"He's the worst singer in the world."

"I'm also better than Phil."

"You're probably also better than Senator Dirksen,"
I said, and David burst out laughing.

"Don't *laugh* at me!" Rhoda said, and turned her
head into Sandy's shoulder.

"I wasn't laughing at *you.*" David said. "My friend
said something funny. If I want to laugh at something
funny my friend says . . ."

"Oh, shut up, David," Sandy said.

"Well, I can laugh if I want to."

"But not at her."

"The hell with her," David said, "I wasn't laughing
at her."

"I *like* to sing," Rhoda said defensively, blowing her nose.

"Fine, honey," Sandy said, "but do it in the shower from now on."

"Do it on a boat sixty miles offshore," I said.

Surprisingly, Rhoda began giggling.

"There," Sandy said.

"Sixty miles offshore," Rhoda repeated, and giggled again.

"She's a manic-depressive," David said.

"Isn't anybody hungry?" I asked.

"I'm famished," Sandy said.

"Then let's all go over to The Captain's for some hamburgers."

Which is what we did.

It rained again on Monday morning, the last day of July.

David's parents were still in New Jersey, so we all went over to his house to listen to records. Eudice had just finished vacuuming the living room. She was well aware that we would make a mess of the place all over again, but she didn't say a word to us, because she was still feeling guilty about her role in having brought David to justice.

David asked us if we would like to hear a talk for which he had got an A in a theory course, and we said absolutely not, and he said Go to hell and gave the talk, anyway. Actually, it wasn't too bad at all. What he did was trace the development from blues and jazz to country western to swing to bop to rock and roll to the new experimental electronic stuff, sounding very much like a college professor, but nonetheless adding new dimensions to something which, until then, we had enjoyed only because the sound appealed to us.

The most important factor in modern pop, he explained, was the development and widespread use of amplification. Volume was essential to the new sound,

sheer loudness that assaulted not only the ears but the
entire human sensory system. It was, in fact, possible
to feel (as he turned up the volume control and caused
Eudice to moan in the kitchen) the buffeting of sound
waves against our bodies, causing an actual vibration
that was something different from the simple audio
experience. For that matter, even my eyes seemed to
be straining forward in their sockets as the sound got
louder and louder, as though they wanted to see what
my ears and my skin told me I was experiencing.

This assault, David explained, was mostly harmonic,
in contrast to earlier music where the melody line was
clearly heard and usually carried by one or another of
the instruments. Today, he said, the melody was over-
powered by background chords. These chord progres-
sions (I had difficulty following him here) were
usually similar and sometimes identical, with the result
that each song had a familiar and comfortable feel to
it. In other words, the effect was one of having heard
any given song many many times before, a repetition
that was hypnotic, demanding from the listener a mini-
mum amount of concentration or involvement.

The dances were elementary, too, a simple response
to the pulsing harmonic background, requiring little or
no concentration, little or no involvement with one's
partner. They were, in fact, onanistic, David said,
which means expressive of nothing but an involvement
with oneself. The new experimental electronic music
was carrying this sense of uninvolvement a step further
because it threw away even the usual chord progres-
sions, substituting instead an erratic series of sounds. It
would become impossible to dance to the music of the
future, he said. It would also become impossible to *listen* to it, except in the way one might overhear a ran-
dom and accidental arrangement of noises.

He explained all this while illustrating his premise
with some really good 45s and LPs. It was fascinating,
most of it, anyway. Even Rhoda seemed pretty im-

pressed by his instruction, although she was a bit ill at ease that first day with us. There was a tight enclosed feeling to the afternoon, the round wood-paneled living room and the fire David had set in the fireplace, the teeming rain outside, the records spinning while he patiently and expertly explained the evolution. Sandy was stretched on the floor before the fireplace like a long tawny cat, wearing tan chinos and a bulky beige turtleneck sweater, barefoot, her blond hair streaming, her jaw propped on one hand. Rhoda sat rather primly at first in the blue wingback chair to the left of the fireplace, only later relaxing enough to tuck her feet up under her.

The rain was relentless. It never varied in its rhythm or its intensity, seemed in fact to add natural conviction to everything David was saying about the sameness of pop music. Rhoda, as it turned out, was a quite bright person who asked intelligent questions, and who smiled in delight each time David satisfactorily answered them. Her smile was a radiant thing, despite the unflattering bands on her teeth. It transformed her entire face, imparting a warmth to it that was totally lacking when she wore her serious, older-party look. She was not an attractive girl, but there was an appealing softness to her, in perfect contrast to Sandy's glittering fine-boned beauty. As the afternoon waned, I found myself liking her more and more, and when David ended his demonstration, I was delighted that Sandy turned the conversation to Rhoda, asking her to tell us all about herself. I thought of that rainy Monday when we had drunk the truth serum, and I wondered now what Rhoda would say. She was under no obligation to tell us anything, of course, except that she was *there,* and the fire was blazing, and the room was warm and cozy, and there was an atmosphere of relaxed permissiveness, the rain outside creating an island within an island, drilling its narrow gray prison bars against each melting window.

"There's nothing to tell," Rhoda said, and blushed. The blush seemed entirely contradictory; I could not imagine it on the face of the girl who had boldly requisitioned Deuce's microphone and drowned the night in horrid sound.

"There's always something to tell," Sandy said. She was eating prunes by the fireplace, lazily dipping her hand into the green Sunsweet box, chewing off the black meat, sucking the pits dry. She had told us the day before that she had been irregular for more than a week now, ever since The Big Rape Scene, when she'd been more terrified than she was willing to admit.

"Well, my mother is dead," Rhoda said, and stopped.

"How did she die?" David asked.

"She drowned," Rhoda said.

"Wow."

"Yes."

"Where?"

"On Martha's Vineyard, five summers ago."

"How old were you?"

"Ten."

"God, that must have been awful," Sandy said.

"Yes. Yes, it was."

"Didn't she know how to swim?"

"Oh yes, she was an expert swimmer."

"Then what happened?"

"Well . . ." Rhoda said, and stopped. "I don't like to talk about it, really."

"Okay," Sandy said, and popped another prune into her mouth. There was something chilling about the way she said that single word, as though she were suddenly excluding Rhoda from our closed society, in effect sending her outdoors into the driving rain. I sensed it, and I know that David did, too. I was surprised, however, to see visible recognition of it crossing Rhoda's face and settling into her serious brown eyes. She hesitated only an instant before speaking again.

Sandy had cowed her with a word, and I almost smiled at the ease of her accomplishment. I restrained myself only because Rhoda, after all, was going to tell us about something very serious and important, the drowning of her mother five years ago on Martha's Vineyard.

"It was a bet," Rhoda said. "My mother made a bet with this man."

"What was the bet?"

"That she could swim out to the sandbar and back without stopping to rest." Rhoda paused. A spark crackled out of the fireplace and onto the living-room rug. Sandy lifted the prune box and then brought it down on the spark, killing it. "There had been a party that night . . ."

"Oh, was it at nighttime?"

"Yes," Rhoda said, "and I think everyone had a little too much to drink. I don't remember very much about it because I was only ten at the time. There was a writer there who had written a bestseller about a man who takes another man's identity, and there was a lyricist who kept using the word 'fantastic' all night long, 'Oh, that's a fantastic roast beef,' or 'Oh, where did you find this fantastic old lamp?' I remember him very distinctly. I don't know how the thing started, I think they were all a little bored. I was in my nightgown already, starting up for bed, going around the room and kissing everyone goodnight. The lyricist was very drunk, when he kissed me goodnight he cupped my behind in both hands and kissed me right on the mouth, smelling terribly of whiskey." She blushed again. Outside, the rain swept in against the windows, driven by a sudden ferocious gust of wind. The eaves of the house creaked. By the fire, Sandy made tiny sucking sounds around her prune pit.

"They were saying that Mother was a great swimmer, and someone remarked that women had more stamina than men, and someone else said women had an extra layer of fat around their bodies, which was what made it possible for them to stay in the water for long periods of time without getting chilled. The writer, I think it was, explained that this was why so many of the long-distance swimmers had been women, like Gertrude whatever-her-name-was who swam the English Channel . . ."

"Ederle."

"Yes, I think that was it. I don't know if what he said was true or not, but I remember the women taking offense at the idea of having an extra layer of fat, and my mother saying—she was very slim and athletic-looking, you see—saying *she* had a lot of endurance and certainly did *not* have an extra layer of fat. All the women in the room said, 'Bravo, Irene,' and that was when the lyricist said Mother's endurance was only a matter for speculation until it was proved. Daddy said that Mother had swum to the sandbar and back without stopping, the sandbar being a half mile offshore, and the lyricist said this was impossible, and Mother said she could do it again anytime, and he said How about right now?

"So that was how it started, I guess. I think they were all sort of restless, there had been a party on Friday night, and another one on Saturday night, and this was Sunday in the middle of August, and it can get kind of dull, I guess, I suppose it had got kind of dull for them. So Mother took me upstairs to tuck me in, and I could hear her changing into her bathing suit in the bedroom next door, and then she came in wearing the suit, a red one, and a short terry-cloth robe over it, and kissed me goodnight. She looked very pretty and very excited. When she kissed me, I smelled the same alcohol on her breath that had been on the lyricist's, but of course she wasn't drunk—she never drank to excess, just to feel happy, she always said. She turned out the light and left the room, closing the door behind her. That was the last time I saw her alive."

Rhoda stopped again and turned her eyes toward the fire, as though trying to find in its turbid flames the words to explain what had happened next on that night five years ago. We were all silent. Sandy sucked on her prune pit once, seemed to sense the sibilant sound was an intrusion, and then simply waited attentively with her head bent, the firelight behind her, the prune pit in her hand.

"The house was empty for a long time," Rhoda said. "They had all gone down to the beach with flashlights to watch Mother as she attempted the swim. I forget how much they had bet, I think it was ten dollars."

"How did she drown?" Sandy said.

"A cramp. At least, that's what they thought. They couldn't know for sure. They said it must have hit her coming back, halfway between the sandbar and the shore. It was Daddy who broke the news to me. 'Your mother is dead,' he said, and I said, 'No, she isn't,' and he said, 'Rhoda, honey, your mother is dead.' " She nodded, and then stared into the fire again.

"That's a rough break," David said.

"Yeah," I said.

"I still miss her," Rhoda said quietly.

"They're pains in the asses," I said, "but I guess you can miss them when they're gone."

"I thought my father was dead for the longest time," Sandy said. "They got divorced when I was a baby, and I grew up thinking he was dead. Then one day this man arrived at the front door of the house and I said, 'Yes, sir, may I help you?' and he said, 'Sandy, I'm your father.' My mother came out of the kitchen and said, 'Get the hell away from her, you bum.' That was the first time and the last time I ever saw him."

"That's worse than if he were dead," Rhoda said.

"He was handsome," Sandy said.

"I often wonder what she was trying to prove,"

Rhoda said. She looked across the room at Sandy. "What could she have been trying to prove?"

"Hey, put on some more music," Sandy said suddenly. "Come on, David, how about it?"

"Okay," David said, and got to his feet.

"You still haven't told us anything about your*self*, though," Sandy said. "Tell us something about yourself."

"Like what?"

"Something terrible."

"I don't know anything terrible."

"Everybody does. Tell her something terrible, Peter."

"I once made Ritz cracker sandwiches out of cream cheese and snot," I said easily, "and gave them to my cousin to eat."

"That's disgusting," Rhoda said, but she giggled.

"What have *you* done?" Sandy asked.

"Nothing."

"Okay," Sandy said, the same single word again, and again she reached into the prune box in dismissal. A look of panic crossed Rhoda's face. She studied Sandy, who had turned her head away and was disdainfully nibbling on the prune. Then she looked at me, hopefully.

I didn't say a word.

David had put on a Beatles LP, and we listened now as "Taxman" flooded the circular living room in the center of the circular house. Outside, the rain drummed its steady accompaniment.

"Well . . ." Rhoda said, but Sandy did not turn to look at her.

"This is the only *really* talented group around," David said, gesturing toward the hi-fi setup.

"I like the Stones better," Sandy said.

"The Stones are derivative."

"But dynamic."

"But derivative."

"What I did once . . ."

"I also like the Yardbirds."

"Second-rate."

"I think they're super."

"What I did . . ."

"Yes, what the hell *did* you do?" Sandy said, turning toward her sharply and abruptly.

"You won't tell anyone?"

"Of course not."

"I . . ."

"Listen to this one," David said as "Eleanor Rigby" started. "This one'll become a classic."

"I spit on my mother's grave," Rhoda said.

"When?" Sandy asked.

"At the cemetery. When everyone else had left. I stayed behind and spit on her grave because she had no right to die that way, no right to leave me all alone." She suddenly covered her face with her hands. "I'm so embarrassed," she said.

"Don't be," Sandy said cheerfully, and then rose and went into the bedroom, where she had left her yellow rainslicker and a brown paper bag. The bag contained two coloring books and a box of crayons she had bought at Mr. Porter's. We spent the rest of the afternoon coloring pictures before the fire.

It was a very good day.

We decided to teach Rhoda to swim.

She assured us there was nothing psychosomatic about her inability to do even the dog paddle, no fear stemming from her mother's drowning, no lingering effects of what might have been considered a traumatic experience. She wasn't afraid of water, she said, nor of the idea of swimming, and in fact never gave very much thought to drowning—although she did often think of her mother's death, but only in terms of an accident and rarely in terms of an accident that took place in water. The only problem about learning to swim, she told us, was her lack of coordination. She couldn't seem to synchronize her arm and leg movements, and as a result she sank to the bottom each and every time she tried. We convinced her this was nonsense, and she agreed to have another go at it, even though she was pessimistic about the outcome.

We went around to The Blue Grotto, where, of course, Violet came out to greet us. She was wearing a white suit with bell-bottomed slacks. Sandy complimented her on the outfit, which I thought made her look like a brewer's horse, and Violet told her she had bought them at a little place on the mainland called Kinship Korner. Sandy promised to look in on the shop, and then she and Violet exchanged some polite chatter about Sunday's party, which I headed off when it started to get to the part about "the horrid little girl who," noticing that Rhoda, ears pricked, was sensitively ready to take offense and possibly burst into tears again.

"Violet, how's chances of renewing our old arrangement?" I said.

"Well, I don't know," Violet said. "You boys hardly spoke to me on Sunday."

"We were very busy," David said. "How about it, sweetheart?"

The "sweetheart" melted her completely. She looped her arm through David's, flabby breast pressed against him, and led him around to the kitchen. He came back some five minutes later, the beer wrapped as usual in his poncho.

"What's in the poncho?" Rhoda asked.

"Shhh," David said.

She looked at him in puzzlement, and then gave a little-girlish shrug and followed us down to my father's boat. Violet came onto the dock with us, helping us to cast off, and waving as we started the engine and moved out. Mr. Matthews' Chris Craft was moored alongside a yacht from Floral Gables. He was aboard

her in swimming trunks and blue cap, cleaning his fishing rods.

"Hi, Sandy!" he shouted as we chugged past, and
Sandy lazily lifted her arm to wave at him.

We hoisted sail as soon as we cleared the breakwa-
ter. There was a good wind that first day of August,
driving bloated white clouds across an azure sky, billowing into the sail, sending us skimming across the
water at close to twenty knots. Sandy was at the tiller,
wearing a new black bikini her mother had bought for
her in the city. Her hair was held at the back of her
neck by a tortoiseshell barrette, and she was wearing
huge sunglasses and a gold heart locket that a boy
from Mount St. Michael's had given her the year before. I was wearing my sawed-off dungarees, which I
sometimes swam in, and David had on a pair of white
boxer shorts with a blue anchor near the change
pocket. He looked positively great. He was handsome
to begin with, of course, but now he had a marvelous
tan, and his hair was much lighter, and his body was
good and tight from all the swimming we did. He also
had this very cool look about him, as though he were a
recording star or something, vacationing incognito on
Greensward and just dazzling anybody who happened
to come into his orbit. It was a good confident look,
and I tried to imitate it sometimes, but it never worked
with me because of my sprouting acne and my dumb
nose.

Rhoda wasn't as white as she'd been that first day
on the beach, but neither was she as tanned as the rest
of us. She was, in fact, an angry red color that combined with her dark hair and eyes to give her a distinctly Indian look. She seemed, too, to be more
*dressed* than the rest of us, wearing her usual one-
piece bathing suit, a blue one this time, the kind of suit
you'd expect a grandmother or a visiting aunt from
Kansas to wear. She seemed thoroughly ill at ease
aboard a boat, ducking in panic each time the boom

swung across the deck, even though it came nowhere close to her. She finally relaxed enough to sit on deck alongside the cockpit. David tuned in his transistor to ABC, and then broke out the beer.

"I don't drink," Rhoda said.

"Beer isn't drinking," I said, and extended an open bottle to her.

"No, thank you. Really."

"We're not boozers, if that's what you're thinking," David said.

"I wasn't thinking that."

"Well, suit yourself," I said, and carried the bottle back to Sandy in the stern. I handed David another bottle and then opened one for myself. The beer was icy cold and sharp. It sent tingling little needles up into my nose.

"What does it taste like?" Rhoda asked.

"Like truth serum," David said, and laughed.

"What do you mean?"

"Private joke."

"Could I taste some?"

"Sure," I said, and handed her my bottle, wiping off the lip for her.

She tilted it to her mouth, took a sip, pulled a face, and spit a mouthful of beer into the wind. "It's *awful*," she said.

"Hey, who's spitting?" Sandy yelled from the stern.

"Oh, I'm sorry," Rhoda said, turning toward her. "I'm terribly sorry, I didn't think . . ."

"That's all right," Sandy shouted. "David, why don't you get her a beer?"

"She doesn't want one!" David shouted.

"What?"

"I don't want one!"

"Why not?"

"I don't like the taste of it!" Rhoda yelled.

"You don't know what you're missing," David said. He brought his bottle to his lips, took a long swallow, said, "Ahhhhhh," and then belched. "Beg your pardon," he said, and grinned, and drank some more.

"It looks good, but it tastes awful," Rhoda said.

"It tastes wonderful," David said, and drained his bottle. "Ahhhh," he said again, and then threw the empty over the side.

"Doesn't that mess up the ocean?"

"It's a mighty big ocean."

"I wish I had a nickel for every beer bottle on the bottom."

"Who wants the tiller?"

"I'll take it," David said, and went back.

Sandy stood up and stretched. "Mmmm," she said, "what a day. Where'd you put my bag, David?"

"In the cockpit," he said, and she went below, out of sight.

"How far is the island?" Rhoda asked.

"Oh, five or six miles, that's all," I said.

"Is the water calm there?"

"Very calm. Nice little cove, no waves."

"Shallow?"

"Yes. Don't worry."

"I was thinking maybe we should have gone over to the bay."

"Too many little kids there."

"You want to learn to swim with a lot of little kids around?" David yelled from the stern.

"No, but . . ."

"You'll like the island, don't worry," I said.

"It won't work, anyway," Rhoda said. "You'll see. I'll sink straight to the bottom. You'll have to rescue me," she said, and giggled.

"It's unnatural not to stay afloat," I said. "Isn't that right, David?"

"Absolutely," he yelled. "If you just relax, you can't possibly sink."

Sandy came out of the cockpit, carrying her beach bag. She took a towel from it, spread it on the deck,

sat, and opened a tube of suntan lotion. She greased
her face and her arms and her chest and the front of
her legs, and then she handed the tube to me, rolled
over on the towel and said, "Would you do my back,
please, Peter?"

"You're so tan," Rhoda said. "Do you still need
that?"

"Keeps the skin from drying out," Sandy said. "Wait
a minute, Peter." She reached behind her and undid
the bikini top, lying flat on the towel, dropping the ties
on either side of her body. "Okay," she said.

I squeezed some of the lotion out onto the palm of
my hand and began spreading it on her back.

"Do you all know each other from the city?" Rhoda
asked.

"No, we met out here," Sandy said.

"You seem like such close friends."

"We *are.*"

"Actually," I said, "David and I have known each
other a long time."

"Where do you go to school?" Rhoda asked.

"Me?"

She nodded.

"The Mercer School. That's on Sixty-first."

"Yes, I know where it is. I live in Manhattan."

"Really? Where?"

"Peter, please pay attention to what you're doing,"
Sandy said.

"Sorry."

"On Eightieth and West End," Rhoda said.

"Would you do the backs of my legs too, please?"
Sandy said.

"May I use some of that?"

"Sure," I said, and squeezed some onto Rhoda's
palm.

"Thank you. Where do *you* go to school, Sandy?"

"Hunter College High."

"She's a genius," I said.

"Oh, sure."

"You are." I paused. "She has an IQ of 157," I said to Rhoda.

"Hey, I wonder whatever *happened* to that thing," Sandy said, raising herself on one elbow, clutching the loose bikini top to her breasts.

"What thing?"

"The questionnaire."

"Did you mail it in?"

"What questionnaire?" Rhoda said.

"Sure, I did. We should have heard by now, don't you think?"

"Sure."

"What are you talking about up there?" David shouted.

"The questionnaire!" Sandy shouted back.

"Cost us three dollars and thirty-five cents each," I said to Rhoda.

"For what?" Rhoda asked.

"A dating service."

"They're going to supply me with a man," Sandy said, and rolled her eyes.

"I still don't understand," Rhoda said.

"It's one of those computer things," I said.

"Oh. They're silly," Rhoda said.

"If you're finished, Peter, please put the cap back on," Sandy said, and then stretched out flat on the towel again, turning her head away from us.

"You want some more of this?" I asked Rhoda.

"Just a little," she said, and held out her hand. I squeezed a blob of it onto her palm, and she spread it on her face, leaving a wide orange streak near her cheekbone. I reached out and smoothed it flat with my fingers.

"Thank you," she said, and blushed.

"Where do *you* go to school?"

"What are you talking about now?" David yelled from the stern.

"Rhoda's school."

"Yeah, man, she's cool," David said, and grinned and snapped his fingers.

Sandy chuckled softly into the towel, her eyes closed.

"I go to Bailey," Rhoda said.

"I know a girl from there. Adele Pierce, do you know her?"

"Is she a junior?"

"I think so."

"She doesn't sound familiar. Is she on the newspaper or anything?"

"Are *you?*"

"Yes, I write a weekly column."

"What about?"

"Oh, mostly think pieces."

"Like what?"

"Oh, I just try to express my thoughts on various things, that's all."

"What's it called?"

" 'Feelings,' " Rhoda said.

"Sounds sexy," Sandy said.

"Oh, no."

"No?"

"No, it isn't, really," Rhoda said.

"Well, I don't think Adele Pierce is on the newspaper," I said.

"Is she on the student council?"

"No, I don't think so. Are you?"

"Yes, I'm my class representative."

"You're both putting me to sleep," Sandy said, and yawned.

"What's going on up there?" David shouted.

"They're swapping biographies," Sandy shouted.

"Did you tell her you're on the swimming team?" David shouted.

I shrugged and said, "I'm on the swimming team."

"Really?"

"Mmm."

"You look like a swimmer."

"How does a swimmer look?" I said, and grinned.

"Oh, I don't know."

"We were undefeated last year," I said.

"He was the only soph on the varsity team, too," Sandy said.

"You must be very good."

"Well, I'm okay, I guess."

"He's the best swimmer I know," Sandy said.

"Will you be teaching me?" Rhoda asked.

"We'll *all* teach you," Sandy said, and sat up. Turning her back to Rhoda, she said, "Would you fasten me, please, Rhoda?" and then said, over her shoulder, "Why do you wear such creepy bathing suits?"

"Me?" Rhoda said, tying the bra top.

"Mmm."

"I don't know." She raised her eyebrows, pulled a small grimace, and then looked down at her suit. *"Is* it creepy?"

"Well, *sure* it is."

"Really?"

"Let's say it's not exactly what they're showing in *Seventeen.*"

"I'm not sure I'm interested in what they're showing in *Seventeen,*" Rhoda said. She looked down at the suit again. *"Is* it creepy, Peter?"

"It's pretty creepy," I said.

"In what way?"

"It's too mature for you."

"It covers too much," Sandy said.

"Well, I have a fair complexion."

"Like Snow White," Sandy said.

"Snow . . . ?"

"The famous Pine Street lawyer."

"What?"

"Skip it."

"I don't understand."

"You should get a bikini," Sandy said.

"All the kids are wearing them," I said.

"Well . . ." Rhoda said, and blushed.

"Yes?" Sandy said.

"Well . . ."

"Say it."

"Nothing."

"You'd look marvelous in one," Sandy said.

"I'd be embarrassed."

"That's ridiculous. Wouldn't she look marvelous, Peter?"

"Sure. All the kids are wearing them, Rhoda."

"Well, I don't think my father would like me wearing a bikini."

"What's he got to do with it?"

"I just don't think he'd like it. He's sort of stuffy about things like that."

"He *looks* at girls in bikinis, doesn't he?"

"Yes, but . . ."

"So?"

"I'm his daughter."

"Everybody's somebody's daughter."

"Except *me,*" I said.

"Yok yok."

"What was that?" David yelled. "Somebody come take this damn tiller."

"Do you want the tiller, Peter?"

"Come on," I said to Rhoda, "I'll teach you how to steer."

"You go do it alone," Sandy said. "Rhoda and I have to discuss her bikini."

I went back to the stern and said, "They're discussing Rhoda's bikini."

"That sounds like an interesting discussion," David said. "Do you want another beer?"

"I would very much like to have another beer," I said. "What's our course, quartermaster?"

"Three-four-zero," David said, "sighting on the fishing boat out there."

"Isn't she underway?"

"Not for the past ten minutes."

"Roger."

"Wilco."

"Over."

"Under."

"Out," David said, and went to get me a bottle of beer.

I felt very good. David uncapped the bottle for me and brought it back to the tiller, and I sat with the polished wood under my right arm, my legs stretched out, the bottle to my lips. From the bow, I heard David laugh and saw Sandy drawing a set of curves in the air with her hands. Rhoda laughed, too, her lips pulling back over her teeth, the metal bands glinting in the sunshine. I studied her carefully and decided she *would* look pretty good in a bikini, Sandy was right. After a while, the fishing boat began moving slowly east, so I sighted on the Coast Guard light marking the shoal, keeping it just off the starboard bow, until Violet's island came into view.

"There she is," I yelled.

"Where?" Rhoda said.

"Dead ahead."

"See her?" David said.

"Yes, now I do."

"Should be there in twenty minutes or so," I said. "Sandy, why don't you get one of those life preservers from under the berths?"

"What for?"

"So we can get Rhoda into the shallow water."

"Good idea," Sandy said, and went below.

There was another boat in the cove when we reached Violet's island.

"We've got company," Sandy said.

"Nuts," I said.

"Do you see anybody?"

"No."

"Where do you suppose they are?"

"Who knows?" David said. "The hell with them. Let's go ashore, anyway?"

"Is it deep here?" Rhoda asked, peering fearfully over the side.

"We can't go in any closer," David said.

"I'm just afraid it'll be too deep."

"Put this on," I said, handing her the life jacket. "You can't possibly sink with this on."

"Are you sure?"

"Positive. And we'll guide you into the shallow water. No, tie it across the front there, that's right."

"I still don't see anybody," Sandy said. "Where are the binoculars?"

"I'll get them," David said, and went aft.

"Do I tie *all* of them?"

"Here you go," David said, handing the binoculars to Sandy, who put them immediately to her eyes. "See anything?"

"No."

"They're probably walking the island."

"Do you think we should go ashore?" Sandy asked.

"Why not?"

"I was thinking of our narrow escape on the mainland."

"What narrow escape?" Rhoda asked, looking up.

"Privileged information," David said. He took the binoculars from Sandy and scanned the beach. "There's a woman's beach bag on the blanket there," he said. "I don't think we have anything to worry about."

"So let's go," I said.

"Do I have to jump in?" Rhoda asked.

"It's really not deep at all," I said. "Just put your left hand on top of the jacket here, to hold it down . . ."

"Why?"

"So it won't hit you under the chin when you jump in."

"Oh. All right. Like this?"

"That's right. And then hold your nose with your right hand. Cross it over your other arm. That's the way."

"Shall I go now?" Rhoda asked, holding her nose between her thumb and forefinger.

"I'll go in first," I said.

"Okay," she said, still holding her nose.

"You can let go of your nose until you're ready to jump."

"Okay," she said.

I went to the side and dove in. The water was clear and cold. I swam underwater some ten feet from the boat, my eyes open, pulling with my arms, keeping my legs tightly together and not kicking, just seeing how much speed I could get up using my arms alone. I surfaced then and pushed the hair out of my eyes and waved to Rhoda where she stood poised on the starboard side amidships.

"Okay," I said, "come on in."

"You're too far away," she shouted.

"Okay, just a second," I said, and breast stroked to about four feet away from the boat. "Okay."

"Will you stay with me when I'm in?" she asked.

"Sure."

"Okay," she said.

"Okay, so come on."

She hesitated a moment longer and then grasped the top of the jacket with one hand, crossed her other arm over it, held her nose, and jumped in. She sank below the surface for only an instant, until the jacket popped her out of the water. I was at her side immediately.

"Here I am," I said.

"Don't leave me," she said. Her eyes were closed.

"You can let go of your nose now."

"Don't leave me," she said again, and released her nose, and opened her eyes.

"Don't worry."

David and Sandy came in with masks and fins and swam to where we were drifting near the boat.

"Everything okay?" David asked.

"Fine."

"Let's swim in."

"Just roll over on your back," I said to Rhoda, "and I'll tow you into the shallow water."

"All right," she said, and obediently rolled over. I crooked my elbow under her chin, keeping her head up and out of the water, and began pulling for shore. David and Sandy dove under together, and surfaced about fifteen feet from where I was still towing Rhoda.

"Same old garbage down here," Sandy said.

"We ought to try the other side of the island," David said.

"Peter, will you need us?"

"No, I think I can manage," I said. I put my feet down, but I still couldn't touch bottom.

"What's the matter?" Rhoda said, alarmed.

"Nothing, just have to go in a little further, that's all."

"We're going to try the other side," David said.

"Okay, go ahead."

"See you later," Sandy shouted.

"Be careful," Rhoda called, which I found curiously touching.

I towed her into the shallow water and then spent the next five minutes coaxing her to stand, assuring her the water would only come to her waist, demonstrating ("See? it only reaches to here on me"), cajoling, and finally losing my temper and shouting, "I thought you weren't afraid of the water!"

"I'm *not!*" she shouted back. She was suspended in the jacket, refusing to lower her feet.

"Well, for Christ's sake, it's only three feet deep here, a *midget* could touch bottom!"

"Don't yell, and don't swear," Rhoda said.

"Put your feet down."

"I will."

"So do it."

"I will, don't worry."

"*Now,* goddammit!"

"Why do you swear all the time?"

"I don't swear all the time, put your goddamn *feet* down!"

"All *right!*" she shouted, and lowered her feet.

"Are you touching?"

"Yes."

"So stand up."

"I will."

"Rhoda . . ."

"I can feel the bottom with my toes," she said.

"That's right, now stand up."

"Are there crabs?"

"Of *course* there are crabs, this is the ocean."

"Do they bite?"

"No."

"What else is there?"

"Barracuda, and moray eels, and giant squids. *Stand up!*"

"You're so masterful," she said, grinning, and stood up. It was the first time I'd ever heard her make a joke. It wasn't such a *good* joke, mind you, but it caused me to smile nonetheless.

"Okay?" I said.

"Yes," she said softly.

"Can you walk in?"

"Yes."

"Okay, so let's walk in."

"All right." She hesitated. "Give me your hand, Peter," she said. "Please."

"Sure." I took her hand in mine. "Don't be fright-ened," I said. "There's nothing to be frightened of."

"I know that."

We waded in toward the shore. She treated the water as though it were an enemy, some strange myste-rious foe that would reach out to swallow her if she did not carefully watch each ominous swell, each deadly surface ripple. When we were some two or three feet from the beach, she ran to the shore and immediately plunked herself down, as if delighted to find dry land beneath her once again.

"Whoo," she said, "that was really exciting."

I didn't say anything.

"I'm sorry I'm such a baby," she said.

"Well," I said.

"But I'll try, Peter." She nodded and then smiled weakly. "Whenever you're ready."

"Well, first take off the jacket," I said. "You can't learn to swim with a life jacket on."

"Some people do."

"Yes, but that's not the proper way."

"Do I have to?"

"If you want to learn," I said. "If you don't want to learn, then leave it on."

"I want to learn."

"Then you've got to take it off, it's as simple as that."

"Okay," she said, and nodded, and began loosening the ties. "We won't go in the deep water, though, will we?"

"No, we'll stay where you can touch bottom."

"Not deeper than my waist," she said.

"Not in the beginning."

"Not until later in the week."

"That's right."

"Or maybe next week."

"We'll see how you do today," I said.

"All right, I'm ready," she said, and dropped the jacket to the sand.

"Now don't go in with the idea of being afraid, okay?"

"I'm not afraid."

"No, not much," I said.

"Well, not much," she said, and grinned.

She was terrified.

We spent perhaps twenty minutes in the shallow water, trying to teach her to kick. I would hold her hands and she would stretch out cautiously on the surface and then begin kicking, only to have her feet and then her legs sink slowly beneath the gentle waves. It was the most incredible thing I'd ever seen in my life, it defied all the laws of physics. We eventually wound up with her arms around my waist, her cheek pressed against my ribs, and she kicking wildly while holding on for dear life, only to have her feet disappear, and then her legs again, it was absolutely supernatural. Finally, she released me, and stood up, and said, "It's impossible."

"Well," I said, beginning to agree with her, "let's rest for a while."

"Take my hand, Peter," she said, and we waded in to shore together.

The island was silent, the cove sat still and smooth, opening into the vaster ocean and the distant horizon and the huge canopy of blue sky and drifting pristine clouds. I lay back with my hands behind my head, and tried to understand why Rhoda couldn't stay afloat.

I was beginning to think she was pretty stupid.

She lay beside me on her side, saying nothing. I glanced at her once and saw that her brow was furrowed, her lips thoughtfully pursed. Then she sighed, and rolled over onto her back, and stared up at the sky, and we were silent for a long time, looking up at the slowly moving clouds.

When she began speaking at last, it was without

preamble, as though she assumed I'd been inside her head and would know immediately what she was talking about. She did not look at me, she continued staring at the sky without following any of the moving clouds, allowing them to pass across her field of vision the way her thoughts seemed to be drifting across the screen of her mind. Her voice was soft, the amorphous clouds above were hypnotic, I closed my eyes and felt the sun on my face. Drowsily, I listened to her, and in a little while I think I dozed and only dreamt her voice beside me going on in its same monotonous tone.

She began by apologizing again for the way she'd behaved, and by admitting she'd lied about her fear of water, but saying again it had nothing to do with her mother's death. The truth of the matter, she said, was that she was afraid of so many things, probably because she felt so out of it most of the time. She couldn't understand this feeling because, after all, half the entire world was composed of people who were twenty-five or younger, which she most certainly was, so why shouldn't she feel right at home? And yet, she always had the feeling instead that a party was going on, and she hadn't been invited. (She'd tried to explore this feeling in her column called "Feelings," and had got letters from a lot of girls at school who thought she was merely a square, which she supposed she was.)

But there was no question in her mind that a party *was* in progress, and that she was out on the lawn only listening to the music and laughter inside. The music at this party was insistent, just as David had described it yesterday, hardly ever melodic, the driving chords and rhythms creating a hypnotic sound to which everybody danced, again as David had described them, in a sort of self-involved trance. No one touched or tried to touch, all the writhing and wriggling was directed at nobody in particular, it all seemed to be part of a show —Come see, come admire, like an exhibition of some kind. (She had written all of this in her column called

"Feelings," Rhoda said, and I thought No *wonder* you got letters.)

Everyone at this party is in costume, Rhoda said, but it isn't a costume ball, they're wearing regular street clothes that only *seem* to be disguises. The girls' skirts are very short, with oh such marvelous colors, bright reds and oranges, greens and blues, pinks and purples, yellows and whites in stripes and polka dots, but they're all combined in such a mad swirl that they seem like *no* color at all. And there are false eyelashes and wigs, flowing falls and sequins, metal skirts and plastic dresses, boots that reach to the calf or the thigh, See me, see me, everybody yells, Look at me, See me! And yet the funny thing, Peter, is that although everybody's so *exposed* and *naked* at this party to which I haven't been invited, there's really *no* exposure at all, do you know what I mean, well, let me explain. (No, I thought, don't bother, you're putting me to sleep.)

Where's the *nucleus,* Rhoda said, that's what I mean. Where's the *person* in all this action and noise, where's the *self* in all this laughter? In fact, why's there so much laughter to *begin* with, and why is it so loud?

The girls never just *stand,* Peter, they move, they're in constant motion before the paintings on the walls, and the sculptures in the corners, lovely girls in motion in a riot of color against the riot of color behind them and around them, laughing and talking to boys whose hair is just as long as theirs, whose slacks are just as tight, moving and laughing *with* the stuff on the walls and in the corners but not *at* it, laughing instead at all the squares who aren't in on this big joke whatever it is. I guess they're even laughing when they take the old pill and go into the next room for some casual intercourse with a stranger or two (She must have blushed here, I don't know, my eyes were closed), and then shake hands afterward and say So long, or How do you do, I don't believe we've met, and then have an-

other good laugh at the newspaper articles that tell
where the action is, because *this* is where the action is.

The sun was hot, her voice was becoming more insistent (a bit hysterical, in fact), she seemed to find in
my silent presence a sounding board for future col-
umns called "Feelings," she put her hand on my arm,
her fingers were cold despite the sun, I think they're
afraid, she said. I think that's why they threw this
party in the first place, and I think that's why it's lasting through the night. But that's exactly why I want to
be invited, Peter! I'm as scared as they are, I want to
be drowned in sound and color, I want to laugh with
them, and dance with them and *move* with them! I
want to *feel* them all around me, I want to *see* them,
yes, see their naked legs and breasts and know that
that's the way I look, too, we're all the same, all of us.
Peter, I *long* to go to that party, but I'm *terrified* of
going to it. I'm such a square, I know, I know. But I
have the feeling that once I get there, I'll *really* become like all the rest, that in our nuclear generation
I'll forget that *I'm* the nucleus and just lose myself in
all the others laughing. I'm such a square, Peter.

I opened my eyes. The sky was still bright with
buoyant clouds, the water still murmured softly in the
cove, but Rhoda's voice beside me suddenly chilled
me, and gooseflesh broke out on my arms and across
my chest.

The summer my mother died should have been the
last summer for me, she said, I should have grown up
fast and all at once, I should have come face to face
with all the loss anyone ever has to experience. But
each year, I seem to lose a little more, more and more
each summer, until I want to shout 'Leave me something, at least please leave me *something*,' until I want
to grab a microphone the way I did at Sandy's house,
and sing out louder than the noise, and thank everyone
for listening, and then smile and tell them who I am,
*me,* 'My name is *Rhoda.*' But I know, I know inside it

isn't any use, I'll have to lose everything sooner or later, and I'll join the others, yes, I'll huddle with them in fear, and the party'll end the minute I get there. *That'll* be the last summer, Peter. Mine and maybe everybody's. And I'm so afraid of winter coming.

"Mmm," I said.

"Yes," she said.

"I've got to be truthful with you," I said. "That's one of the things we don't like about you."

"What is?"

"That sometimes you sound like an old lady."

"Well, sometimes I *feel* like an old lady."

"Then try to *hide* your feelings, will you?"

"I can't."

"Because it isn't much fun to hear somebody making dire predictions."

"You didn't seem to mind when David went on and on about pop music and amplification and . . ."

"That's different, he also played records."

"Well, if Catholics are eating meat," Rhoda said illogically, "and Jews are decorating Christmas trees, where's the meaning?"

"Of what?"

"Of *anything.*"

"The meaning is freedom."

"Oh, baloney," Rhoda said.

"Yes," I said, "freedom, Rhoda. This *is* the nuclear generation, you're right, but it's not the awful thing you seem to think it is. We've finally freed ourselves from the force of gravity, Rhoda, we're on the way to the moon, we're *free!* And in the same way, we're freeing ourselves from suspicion and doubt and ignorance and taboo. Rhoda, you don't have to take *my* word for this . . ."

"Peter, don't you see . . . ?"

". . . ask Sandy, ask David. Rhoda, believe me when I say there's a new and exciting world everywhere around us, and you're simply rejecting it. In fact, Rhoda, *you're* the one who refuses to feel."

"Me? But that's exactly what I've been . . ."

"No, no, I beg your pardon. You said we were all having too much fun and acting as if every day was the Fourth of July."

"I never said that."

"Not in those words, maybe, but what's *wrong* with a little fun, Rhoda? Why don't you join the party?"

"It would be like kissing myself in the mirror," she said.

"Well, what's wrong with *that,* as a matter of fact? You're a pretty girl, Rhoda. If you . . ."

"*Am* I?" she said.

"Of *course* you are. Rhoda, this is a new *era,* people simply can't be bothered with petty restrictions and . . ."

"Am I *really* pretty?"

". . . yes, and foolish prohibitions. Do you suppose it would make a damn bit of difference if you were to strip down naked right here on this beach?"

"Peter, I could never . . ."

"Do you for a minute imagine I'd be shocked?"

"Well, I don't . . ."

"Rhoda, I wouldn't be shocked at all, believe me. I'd *look* at you, yes," I said, and grinned. "But I certainly . . ."

"Well, I wouldn't do it," Rhoda said, and got immediately to her feet.

"Well, don't get excited," I said, "I wasn't suggesting that you actually do it."

"I'm not at all excited."

"Then calm down."

"I'm perfectly calm," she said.

She walked to the edge of the beach, her back to me, her hands on her hips, and stood there looking out over the water. I got up and went down to where she was standing.

"Would you like to try swimming again?" I asked.

"I don't think so."

"Why not?"

"Because I don't want to."

"What *would* you like to do?"

"Go home."

"To Greensward?"

"Yes."

"We can't."

"Why not?"

"Because David and Sandy aren't back yet."

"Then let's go find them."

"They went around to the other side of the island. You can't swim, so how can we . . . ?"

"We can walk," she said.

"Okay, let's walk."

"Fine."

"I'm sorry I upset you," I said. "I didn't realize I was saying anything so terrible."

"It's only that you didn't understand anything *I* said."

"I understood every word of it."

"You were laughing at me all along."

"I was not."

"Inwardly."

"Rhoda, I don't see how you can know that I was laughing inwardly."

From the high ground behind the beach, we could see most of the island where it fell away clear to the pine forest on the opposite end. There was a surf to the north, rolling in against the shore in cresting white breakers. On the eastern end, we could see Sandy and David bobbing on the surface, their faces in the water, swimming back toward the cove where we were anchored.

"They're on their way back," I said. "No sense going after them."

"I'm sorry we argued," Rhoda said.

"That's all right."

"I'll try swimming again, if you want me to."

"Sure," I said.

"Peter . . ."

"Yes?"

"I just get very frightened sometimes. Forgive me."

"That's all right. We all get frightened sometimes."

"But not by the same things."

"No."

"Let's never argue again, Peter," she said, "I'm too fond of you," and suddenly kissed me on the cheek. Blushing, she took my hand, and we started down toward the beach again.

A man and a woman were lying on the blanket, on their stomachs, the man wearing blue trunks, the woman wearing brief red pants. Her back was naked, she had undoubtedly loosened her bra straps. The man had dark curly hair, and the woman had straight blond hair clipped short. The man's hand was on the woman's back. Their heads were very close together. We saw them as we came over the crest of the dune, and we both stopped dead in our tracks, not wanting to intrude, yet at the same time wanting to get back to the beach and the water. The man kissed the woman on the cheek and then playfully slipped his hand inside the back of her pants and moved closer to her on the blanket.

"Oh, this is awful," Rhoda said.

"Shhh," I cautioned.

"Let's walk a little more."

"No, wait," I said.

The woman rolled over and sat up, facing the dune. Rhoda's hand tightened so spasmodically on mine, I thought she would crush my fingers in her sudden grip.

"Oh, Peter," she moaned, and I nodded wordlessly because the blond woman was not a woman at all, the blond woman was a slender, narrow-hipped, well-built young man who moved into his partner's arms now,

gently stroked his face, brought his lips to the other
man's cheek, trailed them over to his mouth, and then
kissed him.

"Oh my God, let's go," Rhoda said.

"No, wait," I said again.

She dropped my hand suddenly, quickly walked
away from me over the dune, and sat apart with her
back to the ocean. I continued watching the men on
the blanket below. They caressed and fondled each
other the way a man and a woman would, oblivious to
their surroundings, very much concerned with the apparent effect of their mutual caresses. I suddenly
thought of what Rhoda had said, *It would be like kissing myself in the mirror,* and then, oddly, all I could
think of was the broken gull on the floor of the forest.

I watched them for a long while.

They broke apart only when they heard Sandy and
David splashing around the point into the cove. The
blond man brought his hand to his hair and patted it
into place, turning his back to me. From the rear, he
looked exactly like a woman again, his back slender
and tanned, his hair coiffed in windblown carelessness.
He was wearing a large ring with a green stone.

"Rhoda?" I whispered.

"What is it?" she said.

"Come on. Sandy and David are back."

"Are . . . *they* still there?"

"The faggots?"

"Yes."

"It's all right now, come on."

She took my hand, and I helped her to her feet.

"Why did you watch?" she asked. Her eyes were
puzzled, her face was squinched up tight, the way it
had been that day on the beach when she'd protested
against our treatment of the gull.

"Because I wanted to see," I said, and we walked
down toward the beach to join Sandy and David.

"If you've seen one regatta, you've seen them all," Sandy said that Wednesday, and promptly trotted Rhoda off to the mainland.

The regatta, as it turned out, was not a very exciting one at all. David and I watched it from the point, together with three dozen other islanders, all of whom began cheering when a boat with a striped blue sail took the lead. But that was the high point of the race. None of the other boats even came close to being in contention, and the outcome was foregone from the starting gun.

Sandy and Rhoda caught the three o'clock boat back to the island and joined us at the point. The race, such as it was, was still in progress, but the number of spectators had dwindled to perhaps a dozen or so, including David and myself.

"Who's winning?" Sandy said.

"Guess," David said, and pointed out to the horizon where the blue-sailed boat was a good hundred yards ahead of the trailing pack.

"How dull," Sandy said. "Wait'll you see what *we've* got. Come on, Rhoda," and they disappeared over the dune.

David began humming. He always hummed very intricately, doing all the parts of whichever symphony happened to be in his head, getting thoroughly involved, and sometimes forgetting there was anyone with him. I kept watching the race and listening to him, trying to place the melody. And then suddenly, he stopped humming in the middle of a passage, surprising me, and said, "You think we should try to lay her, Poo?"

"What?" I said.

*"Lay* her," he repeated.

"Who?"

"Her," he said, and gestured toward the dune.

"Gee, I don't know," I said. This was the first time we'd talked alone together since almost the beginning of the summer, and I felt a little strange. David began humming again. Out on the water, one of the boats heeled way over and seemed in danger of capsizing. The small crowd on the beach let out a yell. I got to my feet and watched as the crew righted her.

"Close one," I said.

"What do you think, Poo?" David asked.

"I don't know."

"I think she'd let us," he said.

"Who?"

"Sandy."

"Oh. I thought you meant Rhoda."

"No. I don't think Rhoda would. Do you?"

"No, I don't think so."

"But I think Sandy would."

"Maybe."

"Well, we can give it a try, anyway," David said.

"Suppose she says no?"

"Well, let's give it a try."

"I'm a little scared to," I said.

"I am, too. But let's give it a try."

"She's liable to get sore," I said. "We've got a pretty good relationship with her. I'd hate to see any-thing . . ."

"She lied about the bird, didn't she?"

"Because she was embarrassed, that's all."

"Still, she lied about killing it."

"What's that got to do with this?"

"Only that she's kept things from us," he said, and shrugged.

"This is different."

"How?"

"It's like plotting against her."

"Okay, why'd she let us feel her up in the movie?"

"I don't know. I think it was the picture."

"No, I think she'd have let us, anyway."

"I don't know."

"Well, let's try it." David paused. "Wouldn't you like to?"

"Yeah, sure, I'd like to."

"She drives me crazy sometimes," he said.

"Yeah. But I like her a lot, Dave, and I wouldn't want to do anything that got her upset, you know."

"We won't, don't worry," David said.

"Also, we'll have to be careful."

"Oh sure, we'll need protection."

"That's not what I meant."

"What did you mean?"

"I don't know, just careful."

"Yes, but we *will* need protection."

"Oh, sure."

"Very definitely," David said.

"Maybe we ought to just forget the whole . . ."

"No, we can get what we need over on the mainland."

"Who?"

"Well, we could go in together."

"You look older than I do," I said.

"Maybe we could draw straws or something."

"I'd be embarrassed going in a drugstore."

"So would I."

"You look older," I said again.

"You *sound* more mature, though."

"You sound very mature, too."

"Well, let's figure it out," David said.

"Look at that goddamn blue boat. Still in the lead."

"Yeah. Does your father use them?"

"Gee, I don't know."

"I think my mother's on the pill," David said. "Why don't you scout around?"

"What do you mean?"

"In his dresser, take a look through the drawers."

"Gee, I'd hate to do that, Dave."

"Would you rather go into some drugstore?"

"Well, no, but . . ."

"Take a look, then. Maybe he's got some."

"Suppose he counts them or something?"

"Why would he do that?"

"I don't know. Maybe they count them." I shrugged. "Look at that damn blue boat."

"Yeah," David said. "Will you scout around?"

"I think maybe we ought to forget the whole thing," I said.

"No, I want to do it."

"So do I, but suppose we go to all this trouble, and Sandy says no?"

"Why would she say no? She loves us. She keeps saying she loves us, doesn't she?"

"Yeah, but she doesn't mean she *loves* us."

"Sure she does."

"Do you love her?"

"Sure I do," David said.

"I mean, *love* her."

"Well, not *love* her. But I do love her."

"That's what I mean. I don't think she loves us, either. I mean, Dave, we've got a really fine relationship here, I'd sure hate to screw it up."

"How can we screw it up? All she can do is say no."

"Yeah, well, I don't like the idea of *that,* do you?"

"She's a nice girl, she'd do it in a nice way."

"I'm not so sure."

"Let's give it a try," David said.

"Well, okay," I said, and sighed.

"You'll look?"

"I'll look."

"And if he hasn't got any, we'll just have to go over to the mainland, that's all."

"Yeah," I said.

The girls came back about twenty minutes later.

Sandy climbed over the dune first in a bikini we had never seen on her before, a wild sort of Gauguin print, skimpy in the top, very brief in the pants. It was Rhoda who thoroughly surprised us, though, Rhoda who stepped through the beach grass shyly and stood above us like a slave girl on the block, waiting to be inspected, dreading rejection, terrified that we'd laugh at her. She looked naked. She was wearing a dark-green bikini certainly no more revealing than Sandy's, and yet I was shocked, and then embarrassed, and then puzzled by my own shock and embarrassment.

"Well, how does she look?" Sandy said, grinning proudly.

"Beautiful," I said.

I thought we did a very good job with Rhoda, if I must say so myself.

To begin with, the new swimsuit brought about a re-markable change, liberating her body (I was alter-nately afraid and hopeful that she would fall com-pletely out of it), and creating what seemed to be a more natural bond between flesh and water, allowing her to *feel* the element through which we were asking her to move. But at the same time, it seemed to free her mind as well, as though by changing her appear-ance, by forcing her into an alien costume, we had also forced her to awaken a dormant skill. We sailed out to Violet's island on the day after Rhoda bought the bi-kini, and the change was apparent at once. The mo-ment we entered the channel, she put on the life jacket without urging or instruction and then grabbed her nose and jumped over the side even before I was in the water. She waited for me to come in, obediently rolled over onto her back so I could tow her into shallow water, ran onto the beach, removed the jacket and dropped it to the sand, and then splashed into the water again, coming in up to her waist and waiting for us to begin the kicking exercises.

We spent all day teaching her, each of us taking turns. It was dreary work. For all her enthusiasm, Rhoda couldn't seem to understand that we didn't want her to bend her legs at the knees, that we were

attempting to teach her the straight-legged kick she
would need for a powerful Australian crawl, so she
kept flapping her feet around in the water as though
her legs were broken.

"She'll catch on," Sandy kept saying.

I wasn't so sure.

To my surprise, though, she kept trying, seeming to
gain a little more knowledge with each attempt, and at
last realizing that we were trying to sidestep anything
as elementary as the dog paddle in an attempt to move
her directly into a strong crawl. Once she understood
this, she straightened her legs ramrod stiff, and kicked
with speed and determination, churning up a furious
froth behind her, beating the water tirelessly.

"I think she's got it," David said.

"By George, she's got it," I said.

Whereupon Rhoda wearily dropped her legs to the
bottom and then, puffing, trudged through the shallow
water to the beach, where she collapsed as though
dead.

"You'll be a good swimmer," Sandy said. "You'll
see."

The very next day, our good swimmer practically had
to be pushed over the side of the boat. She balked at
putting on the life jacket, complained that we had anchored the boat too far from shore, told Sandy to keep
her hands off her when she tried to help with the ties,
and then resisted all our efforts to lure her into the
cove, where I was patiently treading water. When
Sandy threatened to knock her unconscious and *throw*
her in, she grasped her nose with one hand, clung to
the top of the jacket with the other, closed her eyes
and leaped in with her legs apart, as though she were
jumping from a burning building. Once in the water,
she refused to roll over onto her back, pummeling me
with both fists as I came close to her, her eyes closed,
damn near drowning me, and forcing me to remember
all the training I'd ever had in lifesaving courses.

"Slug her," Sandy said.

"Don't you dare!" Rhoda shouted, and opened her eyes.

"Roll over!" I shouted.

We were all in the water now, circling Rhoda like a school of sharks, trying to get close enough to help her.

"Damn it," I said, "roll over!"

"Keep away from me!"

"You stupid idiot," Sandy shouted, "he's trying to get you to shore."

"Don't come near me!" Rhoda yelled, and struck out with her fist again, catching me on the cheek.

"Listen," I said, "you'd better cut that out!"

"Slug her," Sandy said again.

"You louses!" Rhoda yelled.

"Okay, leave her to drown," Sandy said.

"Don't you dare!" Rhoda said.

"Then roll over."

"I'm not a trained animal act," Rhoda said, and we all laughed. The smile broke on her face, metal bands catching sunlight, warmth spreading into her brown and frightened eyes. "Oh, all right," she said, and rolled over.

I towed her toward shore, but the moment we reached shallow water, she stood up and ran for the beach and didn't stop running until she had reached the dune. Standing on the high ground, she looked down at us like the lady of a besieged castle, and shouted, "Don't come up here! You just go swimming around, and leave me alone."

"The girl's crazy," David said.

"Absolutely paranoid," Sandy said.

"The hell with her," I said, and we went back into the water.

In a little while, Rhoda edged her way onto the beach, and then down to the shore. Demurely, she removed the life jacket. She was tanned everywhere, except where her body was newly exposed by the bikini. The white flesh of her belly and the sloping tops of her breasts looked peculiarly vulnerable. Daintily, she stepped into the water.

"I'm ready to try again," she called sweetly.

"Try being a human being, why don't you?" I shouted, and Rhoda giggled. "Oh, okay," I said, and swam in to where she was waiting.

"I'm sorry, Peter," she said, and looked down at her feet.

By the end of the week, we had her swimming around the cove.

Those were golden days.

We took the boat out every weekday morning, blessed with sunshine and fair breezes, feeling healthy and lazy and contented. Rhoda seemed to fit in more easily now, laughing at our jokes, offering nonsense of her own, rarely wincing at our occasional profanities. The boom no longer threatened her; she would laze confidently beside the cockpit, her eyes closed, a curious half-smile on her face, her head thrown back to the sun. She even wore her bikini with casual authority now, her body uniformly tanned, her look of flabby respectability all but gone; she had lost seven pounds in the past week, and she told us she had never felt better in her life.

I was beginning to like her very much.

I don't know what it was.

I found myself staring at her whenever her eyes were closed, finding new and interesting things in her face each time I studied it; the way her brows soared up over her eyes, like quick sure charcoal strokes, her long black lashes, her really marvelous nose with its prominently sculpted bridge tapering gently to a delicate winged tip, her mouth with its full lower lip and deep bow, the freckles that showed on her cheeks even through the tan, it was really a remarkable face. I didn't even mind the bands too much, though I kept wondering what she looked like without them. Once, I stared so hard at her mouth that she opened her eyes as though sensing my penetrating gaze, embarrassing me, and then she smiled and the warmth came over her face again and into her eyes, and she winked at me.

I felt so completely happy last August.

I think I had felt that way only once before in my life, and that was when I was very small, maybe five or six years old. My Aunt Bess owned a little summer cottage in Spotswood, New Jersey, and my parents used to take me out there every weekend. It probably was a dumpy little place, I can't even remember what the inside looked like. It was set in a little clearing surrounded by trees, and it was made of wood, and painted yellow, with small brown-shuttered windows. There was a water pump in the clearing, just outside the kitchen screen door. A big aluminum pot used to sit on a milk crate under the pump's spout. The whole family went out to Spotswood every weekend, dozens of us, aunts and uncles, cousins, even my grandmother before she died. I still can't figure out where we all slept, there must have been a hundred beds inside that tiny house. What I remember most is the activity in the yard. The pump was the nucleus of that house, you see, everything centered and swarmed about it. There was constant traffic through the clearing, screen doors opening and closing, the pump squeaking, water splashing.

I can remember a striped canvas beach chair, and me lying back in short pants, my legs crossed, and bright sunlight pouring into the clearing, and the trees around the yard swaying, looking so very tall. I can remember the hum of the family all around me, buzzing back and forth to the pump, calling to each other, laughing, all in brilliant sunshine, and I can remember feeling warm, and safe, and extremely well-loved.

I felt the same way last summer.

One day, while David and Sandy were exploring the bottom on the western end of Violet's island, I took Rhoda up over the dune and showed her the golden patches of marsh, and then walked her slowly in the sunlight toward the sloping shelf of sand and the luxuriant pine forest. Unlike the one on Greensward, there was a sure sense of life in this forest, the tall healthy trees moving in the wind, the birds navigating flawlessly in and around the branches, the chittering of insects in the undergrowth, the restless motion of small wildlife rattling unseen everywhere. The forest on Greensward was dead. The fire had consumed it, had scorched the ground so thoroughly that even the tentative second growth was stunted and grotesque, as though the earth could nurture only mutants.

"I love it here," I said, remembering my sense of awe that day with Sandy and David, remembering too their curious indifference to what I had found so moving.

"Yes," Rhoda said simply, and squeezed my hand, and then turned to smile at me.

"When you smile . . ." I said, and then shrugged.

"What, Peter?"

"When you smile," I said, "you're beautiful." I felt foolish saying it. I shrugged again.

"Thank you," she said, and then caught her breath as though mustering the courage for what she would say next. Her words surprised me, I knew for certain she was blushing furiously beneath her tan. I heard the slight intake of breath, and then she said, "You're beautiful even when you're not smiling, Peter," and then, immediately, "I'm sorry."

"What for?" I said.

"I didn't mean to embarrass you. I don't know why I said that. I'm sorry."

"I'm not embarrassed," I said, even though I was.

"Peter, listen," she said, "listen to everything."

We listened. We stood holding hands, listening. A blue jay fluttered into sudden flight, cawing into the treetops. Along the length of a fallen branch, a squirrel skittered and stopped, nervously scurried away again, head jerking, and disappeared. A grasshopper leaped into the air at our feet, tumbling like a circus acrobat, and somewhere in the bushes on our right a katydid? a cricket? a cicada? made repetitive scratchy music. Rhoda stood with her head tilted, the dark hair curling in wispy tendrils on the back of her neck, her eyes wide, a lance of sunlight touching her left shoulder. Her hand in mine tightened. I turned her gently toward me, and lifted her face, and kissed her.

She didn't say anything.

She kept her lips together I couldn't feel the bands at all.

We walked deeper into the forest and found a tree with an enormous trunk and sat with our backs against it, still holding hands. I began talking. Rhoda put her head on my shoulder and stared up at me, and I just kept talking and talking. I told her about Spotswood, New Jersey, and about the time we lost my Aunt Mary's dog and had to go searching for him through the underbrush, and how we finally found him whimpering in a tangle of Virginia Creeper, as effectively trapped as if a net had been thrown over him. I told her about my own dog, whose name was Kettle, and which I used to own when we were still living on Seventy-second Street, that must have been about seven or eight years ago. We got rid of Kettle because one night my father came in drunk (I didn't tell that to Rhoda) and tripped over the dog where she was sleeping in the dining room, and she bit him on the leg, and he began kicking her, and I came running from my bedroom crying and yelling for him to stop because I was afraid he'd kill her. That was before I learned my father was a drinking man. I couldn't understand why he'd been so furious with poor Kettle that night, I simply couldn't understand it. (I didn't tell Rhoda any of this, I just told her he'd had a hard day, and was naturally angry when the dog bit him.) My mother called the A.S.P.C.A., and they came for the dog the next afternoon. I was supposed to be at school when they called for the dog, but they arrived at 3:30 on the dot, just when I was getting home, two big men in uniform, come to take Kettle. I began crying. My mother assured me they would take good care of the dog, and one of the men said, "Sure, Sonny, if somebody doesn't claim her in a couple of days, they'll put her to sleep just as gentle," the bastard, though I'm sure he didn't realize what he was saying.

Rhoda listened.

I told her my ambition was to become a lawyer, that once my father had served as a trial juror and when the trial was over—he was not allowed to tell us anything about it while it was in progress—he had come home and described all of the courtroom action (he really told stories beautifully when he was sober—I did not mention that to Rhoda), and then and there I decided what I wanted to do with my life, which was become a famous trial lawyer. I told her that sometimes I stood in front of the mirror in the bathroom and pointed my finger at myself and began asking myself tricky questions. She didn't laugh until I did, and then she laughed only tentatively until she was certain she was supposed to. She kept looking at my face.

I told her, oh Jesus, I told her everything I could think of. I told her about a collection of matchbooks I had once started, and how I saved three thousand and twenty-four of them until I got bored and set fire to them once in the gutter outside our building, just a huge pile of three thousand and twenty-four matchbooks going up in smoke, poof, and again she waited until I laughed before she did. I told her about the gull we had rescued and how it had been the start of a very special relationship between Sandy and David and me, and about how we had trained him, but I did not tell her what finally happened to the gull, and when she asked what became of him, I lied. He flew away, I said. I did not feel strange lying about the gull. What had happened with the gull was something between Sandy and David and me, and I could not have told Rhoda about it without betraying their confidence. I told her that Sandy was one of the greatest girls I'd ever met in my life, and that David was the closest friend I had, even though I never saw him in the city. It was odd, I said, how our friendship survived each winter, how we were able to pick it up again every summer, almost as though we'd never been apart. I told her I suspected the same thing would apply to Sandy, and when she suddenly looked hurt, I said that of course it would apply to her as well, now that she was one of us. I told her how much I loved swimming, and how pleased I was that she was learning so rapidly, how proud it made me feel whenever I saw her actually swimming around the cove. And this was only the beginning, I said (I couldn't seem to stop talking), we were going to teach her how to swim underwater, how to use the snorkel and mask, and she'd be surprised at what was under the sea, an entirely new world that she probably never knew existed. (Are there crabs? she asked. I'm afraid of crabs.)

"Rhoda," I said, "you're afraid of too many things," and I kissed her again, and when we drew apart she looked up at me, and touched my face with her open hand, and then swiftly lowered her eyes.

We left the forest at about three o'clock.

Sandy and David were on the beach, listening to the radio.

When they saw us coming, Sandy sat up and grinned, and said, "You're bleeding, Peter," meaning I had lipstick on my face, which I knew wasn't true because Rhoda wasn't wearing any.

"Gee," I said, "thanks, Sandy," and I jumped on

her where she was lying on the blanket and gave her a
noisy wet kiss on her mouth. Then David and I carried
her down to the water, screaming and giggling and
kicking, and I held her arms while he held her legs and
we swung her out and dumped her. She came up struggling to keep on her bikini top, and then she chased us
all over the beach until we were exhausted.

Rhoda sat on the blanket, watching us.

Sandy's caller opened the telephone conversation in
Spanish.

*"Buenos días,"* he said.

*"Buenos días,"* Sandy replied.

*"Está Sandra, por favor?"* he said.

*"La soy,"* Sandy said in hesitant Spanish.

*"Ah, bueno!"* the caller said. *"Aquí el Señor Aníbal
Gomez. Su número de teléfono . . ."*

*"No hablo español bien,"* Sandy said.

*"Sí, verdad,"* Gomez said. *"Usted no habla más que
el inglés, el chino, y el griego,"* he said, and laughed.

*"Por favor, puede usted hablar inglés?"* Sandy said.

*"Sí, sí,"* Gomez said, "I am sorry to speak Spanish,
when it informs me here that you speak fluent Chinese
and Greek."

"What?" Sandy said.

"I have received your number," he said, "and so I
am calling."

"What?" she said.

"It says that we have been chosen," Gomez said.
"By the machine."

"Oh!" Sandy said. "Yes, yes, of *course.*"

"Ah, now you understand?" Gomez said.

"Yes, yes, certainly," she said, and covered the
mouthpiece with one hand and said, "It's my date."

"What?" David said.

"Shhh," she warned, and then said, "Yes, Mr.
Gomez, how are you?"

"I am fine, and you?" he said.

"Fine, thank you."

*"Bueno,"* he said. *"Sandra, es usted una morena?"*

"I beg your pardon?"

"Your hair is black?"

"Oh, yes, yes, it is," Sandy said.

*"Bueno.* You also have blue eyes?"

"Yes, I have."

*"Bueno.* The machine says you wish to meet a Puerto Rican gentleman, which I am."

"That's right."

"Who is very bright like you, which I am."

"Good," Sandy said.

"Also, I am five feet seven and one inches tall, with black hair and brown eyes, is that true?"

"That's certainly true," Sandy said, and stifled a giggle.

"How tall are *you?"*

"Five-four," Sandy said.

"I wish to see you," he said.

"Fine," she answered. "When?"

"I had hoped this Saturday night, if that would be nice for you."

"That would be very nice," she said, and again covered her mouth to suppress a giggle.

"Where is this number?" he asked.

"Well, I'm on Greensward," she said, "but there's not too much to do here. Perhaps I can meet you on the mainland."

"Please speak more slowly," he said.

"The mainland. Do you have a car?" she asked.

*"Sí, tengo un carro.* Yes, I have."

"Well, fine," Sandy said, "get a pencil, and I'll tell you how to get here."

"More slowly, *por favor,"* he said, and she repeated what she had just said, and went on to give him a detailed auto route from Manhattan. They then spent another five minutes settling on a time and place to meet over on the mainland, deciding on 6:30 at the ferry slip, and then Gomez said, "I look forward to it, Sandra," and Sandy said, "Me, too, Aníbal," and he said, "Good," and hung up.

"Well, I guess I have a date for Saturday night," Sandy said. She was lying full length on her bed, and she rolled over now to replace the telephone receiver, and then began giggling. Rhoda, who was reading in the floppy armchair opposite the bed, looked up from her paperback and said, "What?"

"I said I have a date for Saturday night."

"Who with?" Rhoda said, and I realized she hadn't heard a word of the telephone conversation. David and I, who had been playing chess on the floor, had of course heard only Sandy's half of the conversation, so she promptly filled us in, using a Spanish accent that was hilarious.

"You're not *going*, are you?" Rhoda asked, appalled.

"Of course I am!"

"I don't think you should," Rhoda said.

"Why not?"

"It isn't right."

"Here comes Mother Hubbard again," Sandy said, and rolled her eyes.

"Well, it *isn't* right," Rhoda insisted. "That poor man is probably lonely and . . ."

"Rhoda, let's not make him into one of the hundred neediest, okay?"

"I don't think you should go, either," David said.

"What!"

"For different reasons, though," he said, smiling. "To begin with, he's expecting someone who's twenty years old. You're only . . ."

"I can pass for eighteen," she said. "I'll wear my mother's wig."

"Your mother's wig is red. You described yourself as . . ."

"That's right, but I'll wear a kerchief over it. He'll never know the difference."

"I've got a better idea," David said, and again he smiled.

"What's that?"

"Send Rhoda in your place."

"*Who?*" Rhoda said.

"Hey, that's . . ."

"Absolutely *not!*"

"But Rhoda, it's perfect!" Sandy said, leaping off the bed and rushing to where she sat. "You're the right size, you're the right coloring, you're the right *everything!* David, that's a marvelous idea!" she said, and threw her arms around him.

"That's a *lousy* idea," Rhoda said. She closed the paperback book with a small flourish, put it back into the bookcase with great care, and then said, "Anyway, my eyes are brown."

"We'll tell him the machine made a mistake."

"And I don't speak Chinese or Greek."

"Neither do I."

"Neither does *he,* for that matter," David said.

"I don't know any Spanish, either."

"He speaks perfect English."

"Oh yes, he *sounds* as if he speaks perfect English."

"I was exaggerating his accent. He speaks fine. In fact, he sounded very nice."

"Then why do you want to make a fool of him?"

"I don't. I'm after the machine."

"Why? What'd the machine do to you?"

"I don't want to be computerized," Sandy said.

"Then why'd you send in the questionnaire?"

"To screw up the machine," Sandy said.

"But now you're going *along* with the machine."

"How do you figure that?"

"By keeping the date."

"No, I'm screwing up the machine," Sandy said.

"I don't like that kind of language, Sandy," her mother called from the other room.

"Sorrrrry!" Sandy sang back. "I'm screwing up the goddamn machine," she whispered to Rhoda.

"You're screwing up a human being," Rhoda said. "You're screwing up Mr. Aníbal Gomez, who doesn't speak English too well, and who thinks you're a lonely person like himself who wants to meet . . ."

"I said I don't want to hear that language!" Sandy's mother called again, a definite note of warning in her voice this time.

"I *am* a lonely person," Sandy whispered.

"Oh, Sandy, please."

"Where's your sense of adventure?" David said.

"I haven't got any," Rhoda replied. "And even if I did, I wouldn't want to get involved in this . . . double cross."

"It's nothing of the sort," Sandy said. "The machine thinks I'm one person but I'm really another, so I'm sending along a totally *different* person to further confuse the machine."

"People aren't machines!" Rhoda said. "Aníbal Gomez is a *person*."

"How do we know *he* didn't lie to the machine, too? He may turn out to be an old man of sixty with his *teeth* falling out!"

"Fantastic!" David said. "A *triple* cross!"

"I don't want any part of it," Rhoda said. "Period."

"Okay," Sandy said, and walked out of the bedroom.

We went down to the boat at around one o'clock.

Sandy wasn't speaking to Rhoda, and Rhoda was visibly hurt, and I didn't know quite what to do about it. I was very fond of Rhoda, but I *did* feel an allegiance to Sandy as well, and frankly I couldn't see why Rhoda was making such a fuss over a simple practical joke. In fact, David's idea seemed like a very good one to me. Besides, I *had* helped Sandy fill out the questionnaire and I *did* have a sizable investment in the outcome; three dollars and thirty-five cents does not grow on bushes where I come from. So Rhoda's attitude seemed indefensible, and I could understand Sandy's anger, though I did think she was carrying it a bit far by not speaking to Rhoda and causing a very strained atmosphere aboard the boat.

David came up with a new idea as we got underway, a suggestion I was sure Rhoda would welcome enthusiastically. He thought we should *all* keep the date with Gomez, which would provide Rhoda with the protection and camaraderie she might need, as well as enabling us to observe Gomez's reactions at close range. Rhoda, sulking by the cockpit, squinting into the wind, said, "If *anything,* that's a *worse* idea than the original one," and David shrugged and looked at me, and I looked back at him, and then glanced at Sandy who was handling the tiller with all the warmth of a U-boat commander. I shrugged back at David, and we hoisted sail and headed for Violet's island.

Rhoda kept looking at me as though anticipating support of some kind, but I still didn't know quite what to do. So we had a jolly trip out to the island, Rhoda sulking, and Sandy fuming, and David and I trying to make jokes at which only the two of us laughed, oh, it was a very pleasant voyage indeed. When we got to the cove, it became apparent that Sandy's freeze was only going to increase in intensity as the afternoon wore on. To begin with, she refused to come into the water. Then, when I asked Rhoda whether she was ready for her next swimming lesson, Sandy remarked, "She'll never learn. She's uncoordinated," and Rhoda burst into tears.

"Now, listen," I said, "this has gone far enough."

"I can't help it if I don't want to hurt that poor man," Rhoda blubbered.

"Who's trying to hurt him?" Sandy shouted.

"*You* are!"

"I am not! Peter, tell her I don't intend hurting him!"

"She doesn't intend hurting him, Rhoda. Now stop crying."

"Then why does she want me to go out with him and pretend I'm her and make fun of him?"

"I don't want you to make fun of him! It's only a joke, haven't you got a sense of humor?"

"I have a very fine sense of humor," Rhoda said, sobbing.

"Here's a handkerchief," David said, "don't gook it all up."

"I write jokes in my column," Rhoda said, blowing her nose.

"I'll bet they're side-splitting," Sandy said.

"Peter, tell her to stop."

"Stop it, Sandy, can't you see she's upset?"

*"She's* upset? How about *me?"*

"You're *both* upset," I said.

"You'd think I suggested something heinous!" Sandy shouted, pronouncing it "high-nous."

*"Hay*-nous," David corrected.

"Don't *you* start!" Sandy shouted.

"Everybody shut up!" I shouted.

"I've never been out with a boy in my life!" Rhoda shouted.

"All right, everybody, shut up!" David shouted.

"We said we'd go with you, didn't we?" Sandy said.

"Yes, but . . ."

"You think we'd let you go alone?" David said.

"No, but . . ."

"So what are you afraid of?"

"Don't be so afraid of life, Rhoda."

"This is only a joke, Rhoda."

"We'll tell Gomez all about it when the night's over."

"We'll all have a good laugh together."

"Including Gomez."

"We'll tell him what a good joke it was."

"He sounded very nice on the phone."

"He's driving all the way out here, Rhoda, he must be very nice."

"Am I really uncoordinated?" she asked, sniffling.

"No, you're swimming beautifully. Isn't she swimming beautifully, Peter?"

"Beautifully," I said.

"Will you go, Rhoda?" Sandy asked.

"Will you come with me?"

"Absolutely."

"And you'll stay with me? You won't leave me alone with him?"

"Not for a minute."

"And you promise we won't try to make a fool of him?"

"Why would we want to make a fool of him?"

"I don't know, but . . ."

"Say yes, Rhoda."

"I . . ."

"Say yes."

"All right," Rhoda said, "but . . ."

"You're a darling," Sandy said, and hugged her. "Come on, let's get in the water. I want to show you something."

She spent the entire afternoon with Rhoda in the shallow water, painstakingly instructing her in the use of the mask and snorkel, showing her first how to wash the inside of the face plate with spit so that it wouldn't cloud underwater, and then showing her how to fit the mask to her face, and how to quickly lift it to release any water that might seep in, showing her how to pop her ears in case she ever went into deeper water and the pressure started to build, showing her how to blow water out of the snorkel, working patiently and calmly and gently, allowing Rhoda to progress at her own speed, without any insistence, until she was swimming freely around the cove, face in the water, and at last taking a few tentative dives with Sandy, who held her hand while they explored the bottom together.

On the boat, David said, "Did you look?"

"What do you mean?"

"Did you check out your father's stuff?"

I hesitated. The thought of going through my father's belongings had scared hell out of me. I had tried to bring myself to do it, telling myself there was nothing to fear. But each time I started into the bedroom, I had the feeling I might discover something that would shock me, and I didn't want that to happen. So I hadn't done it. And here was David, asking about it.

"Did you?" he said again.

"Yes," I said. This was the first time I'd ever lied to him in all the time I'd known him. I felt as if he could see clear into my skull, as if he knew instantly that I wasn't telling the truth.

"And?" he said.

"I guess he doesn't use them," I said.

"Mmm," David said, and shaded his eyes to watch the girls as they surfaced. "I want to get moving on this," he said.

"Yeah, me too," I said.

"We'll be on the mainland Saturday night," David said, "when we go to meet Gomez. We'll have to get them then."

"Okay," I said.

"It ought to be a riot," David said.

"Well, I don't think we ought to make fun of him," I said.

"No, no, of course not," David said.

"I mean, we promised Rhoda."

"Sure." Looking out over the water, he said, "She's really coming along nicely."

"Mmm."

"You still feel the same way?"

"What do you mean?"

"About her."

"What do you mean?"

"That there's no chance."

"Oh. I don't know."

"She's got great tits," David said.

"Yes," I said.

"Is something the matter?"

"No."

"You sound funny."

"No. I'm okay."

"If you're worried about Saturday night . . ."

"No, no."

". . . I'll do the asking."

"What do you mean?"

"If you come in with me, *I'll* do the actual asking."

"Oh. Okay. Sure."

"Then maybe we can try it sometime next week."

"Okay."

"Right here. This'd be a good place, don't you think?"

"Yes," I said.

"You sure you're all right?"

"Yeah, sure," I said.

That was on Wednesday.

By Friday, we had Rhoda diving from the boat in the deeper water just outside the cove and spending half the afternoon below the surface. The water was exceptionally clear, and very warm now that it was August, but otherwise as disappointing as the cove itself had been, with little or no marine life to observe.

Our routine was unvaried.

We floated on the surface, masks in the water, until one or another of us spotted something that looked interesting. A finger pointed, a head nodded, the original discoverer jack-knifed into a surface dive and headed for the bottom, the rest of us following in formation. A glistening explosion of tiny bubbles trailed behind the kicking fins, I could see Sandy's long blond hair flowing free in the water like a live golden plant, Da-

vid's powerful arms thrusting, Rhoda beside me. And
then the discovery, whatever it was, a gleaming bottle
top, a fishing lure and broken line tangled into a
smooth piece of driftwood, a lumbering horseshoe
crab, a school of tiny shiners, a pink bathing cap. Each
new discovery delighted Rhoda; she would nod her
head vigorously and then break into a wide grin
around the snorkel mouthpiece, scaring me to death
each time because I kept thinking she'd take in a
mouthful, and choke, and panic, and forget everything
we'd taught her.

Our underwater world was silent and exclusive.

We moved through it like conspirators.

Aníbal Gomez looked like an accountant.

He was wearing a simply tailored brown tropical
suit, a pale-beige shirt, and a dark-brown tie. His socks
were brown, as were his shoes, and he wore brown-
rimmed spectacles. We identified him on the dock at
once, the only individual there that Saturday night who
looked even remotely civilized, standing apart from the
ferry company personnel, who wore dungarees and
chambray shirts, and the islanders coming and going in
varied colorful and sloppy attire, and the sports fisher-
men in white shorts, windbreakers, and yachting caps.

The four of us had dressed for the occasion, too,
though certainly not as elegantly as Gomez. Sandy had
put on her mother's red wig, not in any attempt to further baffle her Selecta-Date suitor, but only as defense
against possible recognition by any of the townies who
had chased us in July. She and Rhoda were both wearing thonged sandals and crisp cotton shifts, hers yellow, Rhoda's blue; they both looked very pretty. David
and I were wearing pressed khakis, sports shirts and
jackets. The jackets had been put on under duress.
Sandy had suggested that we wear ties, too, but we'd
absolutely refused and threatened to blow the whole
evening if she insisted, which she did not. As we came

off the ferry and onto the dock, David whispered, "There he is."

"Is everybody ready?" Sandy asked.

"I'm terrified," Rhoda said.

"Let me handle it," Sandy said.

"I feel like a hitchhiker with three friends hiding in the bushes."

At the far end of the dock, Gomez stood watching the passengers as they unloaded, waiting for his date.

"Here goes," Sandy said, and walked to him with her hand outstretched. Clearly expecting a brunette (On the phone, he had specifically asked about the color of her hair), Gomez was startled to see a red-head approaching him and offering her hand. He was a short person, coming eye to eye with Sandy, who, in the wig, looked easily as old as he did. His face was smooth and very white, his eyes brown. A gold tooth showed at the side of his mouth when he opened it in surprise. Tentatively, he took her hand.

"I'm Sandy," she said, shaking his hand vigorously, and then dropping it. His eyes widened behind their glasses when he saw Rhoda and David and me walking over, and he seemed utterly baffled for an instant, seemed in fact as if he were about to run clear off the dock and all the way back to Manhattan. "Let me explain," Sandy said quickly. "This is my friend Rhoda, she's your date for tonight, she's the girl who filled out the questionnaire."

"But . . ." Gomez said.

"She's very shy," Sandy said, "which is why she used my name."

"*Ah, sí, lo entiendo,*" Gomez said. He turned to Rhoda. "How do you do?" he said. "I am Aníbal Gomez."

"How do you do?" Rhoda said shyly.

"But your eyes are not blue," he said.

"She used my eyes," Sandy said quickly.

"Oh."

"Yes, I'm sorry," Rhoda said.

"That is all right," Gomez said. He looked her over carefully. He still seemed on the edge of panic. Every thought flashing through his mind appeared instantly on his face, as though he were incapable of the slightest subterfuge. His eyes behind their magnifying lenses, his sensitive mouth, even his nostrils expressed doubt, and then suspicion, and then further confusion, and finally resignation. He had come all the way from Manhattan, his look clearly stated (he would have made a terrible spy), and for better or worse he would see this thing through, not with Sandy, it seemed, but with Rhoda instead, who claimed to have filled out the questionnaire, and who certainly appeared to be somewhere between nineteen and twenty with dark black hair, as she had claimed, but not with blue eyes, well, he would have to forego the blue eyes (all of this appearing in sequence on his face, he was about as inscrutable as a sparrow), and certainly of ample build, as she had promised, with very large *tetas* like Puerto Rican girls, and truly about five feet four inches tall, though she did not appear at all Oriental, but perhaps the Jewish part of her ancestry had dominated the Eastern influence, well, he would have to make the best of it. And then his transparent system of telegraphy flashed fresh puzzlement into his eyes and onto his mouth and caused his nostrils to twitch again, and we could clearly read his new concern: Who Are These Two Boys With Her?

"These are friends of yours?" he asked.

"Yes. They're with Sandy," Rhoda said.

"They're with me," Sandy said.

"Ahh," Gomez said. They seem very young for her, his face telegraphed, but perhaps there is a shortage of available men on the island. "Well," he said, "are we to be together?"

"I thought it might be nice," Rhoda said.

"Ahhh," he said, and his mouth turned slightly

downward, and his eyes grew sad behind their spectacles, and he sniffed. "Ahh, well, if you wish," he said.

The first thing David and I did was go to the drugstore. It was painless. David asked for a tube of hair cream and a dozen prophylactics (which I thought excessively ambitious), and then we went outside to where Gomez was waiting with the girls, and David made a joke about greasy kid stuff, which Gomez didn't get. I was finding it more and more difficult to keep from putting him on, even though we'd promised Rhoda. He had no sense of humor, not the tiniest shred. His initial surprise and confusion had given way to an amiable submissiveness; he was willing to let us call the shots, and meekly followed us through the town, waiting outside the drugstore at our suggestion, accepting the idea of window-shopping before dinner, approving our choice of a restaurant and even, once we were seated, supplying coins for the juke box selections *we* made.

The restaurant, one of the least objectionable in town, was on a side street across the way from Woolworth's, its decor consisting largely of red leatherette booths and checked tablecloths. But it was clean and American, meaning it served a bland cuisine designed to offend no one. Gomez suggested we have a cocktail before dinner, but since we were all underage and didn't need the embarrassment of being asked for identification, we all came up with various excuses which he accepted without question. Rhoda said she didn't drink, which was the truth. Sandy said she didn't feel like one right now, perhaps a brandy after the meal. David and I said we had each had two doubles before leaving the island, and didn't want to chance another. But we all urged Gomez to have one if he wished, and he ordered a scotch and water, and then lifted the drink when it came and said, "*Salud,* Rosa."

"It's Rhoda," she said.

"Rhoda? Ahhh, Rho*da*. Ahhh, ahhh," Gomez said and drank.

There was something terribly old-world about Gomez, something that spoke gently of haciendas and guitars, mantillas and black lace fans, soft Mediterranean breezes. The truth of the matter, however, (as he revealed it in an autobiographical monologue directed chiefly at Rhoda, catching us only tangentially as it were, but almost putting us to sleep nonetheless) was that he was born and raised in a Puerto Rican village named Las Croabas, thirty-six miles from San Juan, where his father was a poor-but-honest (ho-hum) fisherman except during the cane season when he took to the fields. Aníbal (it was a difficult name to pronounce, so we immediately bastardized it to Annabelle) had lived in a wooden shack near the beach, and his only American contact had been with adventurous tourists who drove up from San Juan and rented his father's boat for snorkeling expeditions. He had usually accompanied his father on these trips, taking the divers out to Cayo Lobos some three and a half miles offshore, and then watching the tall, elegant, rich people frolic in the water while the boat drifted and he ate his noonday meal of cheese and bread. Seven years ago, he had come from Puerto Rico to live with an aunt in Spanish Harlem. His father had by that time taken a job as a beachboy at the Caribe, and was earning more money than he'd ever earned from his combined fishing and cane cutting activities.

"Anything by The Stones there?" Sandy asked David.

"I don't see anything," David said. "Here's a new Blues Project, though."

"Oh, good, play it," she said. "Do you mind, Annabelle?"

"No, not at all," he answered, "but it is *Aníbal*. The accent is on the second syllable, Ah-*nee*-bal, do you see? not Annabelle. Annabelle is a girl's name, no?"

Well, he went on to say, he was still living in Spanish Harlem, where he had managed to avoid the evil of narcotics addiction (those were his exact words) and where he worked during the day at a liquor store that had been at the same location for twenty-three years, while meantime studying accounting (we knew it!) at Columbia University three nights a week.

"You want to be an accountant, is that it?" Sandy said.

"Yes, of course," Aníbal said, and smiled.

"Why don't you have another drink, Annabelle?" David said.

"If no one minds."

"No, go right ahead."

"But it is Aníbal," he said, and again smiled.

"*Ah*-nee-bal," Sandy said, misplacing the accent.

"No, no," Aníbal said, laughing, "you make it sound like '*animal*.' No, no, it is Ah-*nee*-bal."

"Well," Sandy said, and shrugged, and smiled.

"It is difficult, I know," Aníbal said, and then ordered another scotch and water.

He then asked Rhoda about the masters degree Sandy had concocted for the questionnaire. Rhoda was supposed to be twenty years old, of course, which made a masters virtually impossible unless she had graduated from college at the age of eighteen or thereabouts, which age she wasn't about to reach for another three years. Trapped in Sandy's original lie, Rhoda blushed and said, "Oh, yes, *that*," and glanced at Sandy, who immediately said, "She's very shy. Her masters is in sociology."

"Ahh, yes?" Aníbal said, and it was my guess he didn't know what sociology meant. His fresh drink arrived. He raised the glass, again said *"Salud"* to Rhoda, including us in a retrospective nod, and drank. It was then, I think, that we decided to get him drunk.

I don't know whose idea it actually was. I only know that the notion was suddenly there, flashing between Sandy and David and me with the same electrical intimacy we had generated that night of the firehouse dance. Our eyes met. There was no need to nod, or smile, or offer acknowledgment of the idea in any way. It was simply there, we felt it taking shape and gaining power, it surged around and over the table, it was as if we had our arms around each other and could feel each other's pulse beats: we would get Aníbal Gomez drunk.

We did not, however, reckon with Rhoda, who seemed to sense our scheme the moment it was hatched. When Aníbal finished his second scotch, Rhoda immediately suggested that we order, but David said, "Perhaps Annabelle would like another drink."

"I'm starved," Rhoda said, and shot a pointed glance at me.

"Well, we have loads of time," Sandy said, "there's really not much to do here in town."

"Except eat the big dinner," I said, referring of course to the Hemingway story and pleased when David got the allusion and nodded.

"Sure," Sandy said, "have another one."

"Only if you join me," Aníbal said.

"We're ahead of you already," David said.

"If Rhoda is hungry . . ."

"I'm *starved*," Rhoda said again, and again glanced meaningfully at me.

"Then . . ."

"Miss," David said, calling the waitress, "another scotch and water here, please."

"No, truly . . ."

"Make it a double," Sandy said, and then smiled at Aníbal and whispered, "Save us the trouble of ordering another one later."

"Sure, live it up a little," David said. "What the hell, you came all the way out from the city."

"But if Rhoda feels . . ."

"How was the traffic coming out?" I asked, changing the subject.

*"Pués, ni malo, ni bueno,"* Aníbal said. "So-so."

"Where'd you leave the car?"

"In the lot. Near the ferry."

"Here's your drink," Sandy said. *"Salud."*

*"Salud,"* Aníbal answered, and drank. He shrugged at Rhoda, who now had a pained expression on her face.

"I'd like to see a menu," she said. "Peter, would you ask the waitress for a menu?"

"Well, there's no hurry," I said. "Annabelle's still drinking."

"Peter . . ."

"Rhoda, there's no hurry," I said, and looked her straight in the eye.

"You promised," Rhoda said, meeting my gaze.

"Eh?" Aníbal said, and smiled.

"Don't blow it, Rhoda," David warned.

"Eh?" Aníbal said again.

"Rhoda's on a diet," Sandy explained hastily.

"Why do you need a diet?" Aníbal asked gallantly. "You are very slim and nice."

"Thank you," Rhoda said.

"You are *all* very nice," Aníbal said, and drank again. "Are you sure you will not join me?"

"No, but go ahead," David said.

"Miss, another double," Sandy said.

"No, please . . ."

"Drink up, drink up," David said.

Aníbal drained the glass. Rhoda, fully aware of what was happening now, raised her eyes plaintively to mine, and I read in them for only an instant a sure accusation of betrayal, which I chose to ignore. If Aníbal *felt* like drinking, how were *we* doing anything so terribly wrong? I looked at Rhoda one last time, and turned away. On the seat of the red leatherette booth, Sandy took my hand in hers.

There were some swift currents swirling around that booth for the next ten minutes, and I began to get a little dizzy trying to cope with them all. Aníbal had completely entered into the spirit of the bacchanal now, recalling whatever annual feast it was the natives celebrated in the streets of Las Croabas on Holy Saturday, voluntarily ordering another double scotch, and swilling the stuff like water. His eyes were bright behind their spectacles, and I had seen that same brightness often enough in my father's eyes to know that complete stupor was only a hairsbreadth away. I began to feel guilty about my role in getting him drunk. That was one of the currents, and it had nothing to do with anything Rhoda had said, nor anything to do with the signals her eyes had flashed. It had only to do with my father. It had only to do with this Puerto Rican connoisseur of good scotch who, like my father, might come to me in a predawn nightmare, and awaken me, and sit by my bed, and moan in inebriated cadence, "Oh, Peter, oh, Peter." I suddenly remembered that day in the forest when Rhoda and I had listened to the sounds everywhere around us, and where I had lifted her lips to mine and kissed her without feeling even a suggestion of the metal bands. I thought of Spotswood, New Jersey, and of a clearing in bright sunshine, and a small boy in a striped beach chair, bare legs crossed, had my father been a drunk even then? it did not seem possible. Sandy's hand over mine was warm and restless. I knew she was also holding David's hand, and I remembered that night in the movie theater, and I thought of what she had admitted on the walk to the ferry, and of the townies wanting to get at her, and of David's plans for her, and I suddenly got very excited and squeezed her hand tightly, and looked into Rhoda's eyes, and for some reason had the strangest feeling I was watching Rhoda on film, as if the reality of Rhoda was rapidly fading, the reality was only Sandy's hand and the promise beneath the cotton shift, the reality was here on this side of the table while the film, the illusion, was there across from us, Aníbal putting his hand over Rhoda's on the tabletop and whispering, "Rosa, you a pretty *muchacha,* you know what that means? It means a pretty girl, Rosa."

"Rosa ees a pretty gorl, *sí,*" Sandy mimicked.

"A *muchas* pretty gorl," David said.

"No," Aníbal said, "no '*muchas,*' what we say is '*muy,*' we say '*muy linda,*' that means 'very beautiful.' "

"Thank you," Rhoda said.

"*De nada,*" Aníbal said.

"*Muy linda,* that ees you, Rosa," Sandy said.

"There is a rose in Spanish Harlem . . ." David sang.

"Ahhh, *sí,* you know that song?" Aníbal said.

"Ahh, *sí,* I knew it *muy bien,*" David said.

"*Muy bien,* very good," Aníbal said, and his elbow slipped off the table and he almost hit his chin on the tabletop. He burst out laughing, and I was suddenly frightened.

"Let's eat," I said, "I think we should eat now."

"No, Annabelle wants another drink," Sandy said.

"Annabelle enjoys *el boozo mucho bien,*" David said.

"No more whiskey," Aníbal said, "I may get drunk."

"He *may* get drunk!" Sandy said, exploding into laughter.

"Tell us more about Spanish Harlem," David said. "Tell us about the roses there."

"Tell us about the *rats* there," Sandy said.

"How about the rats *here?*" Rhoda said, suddenly and sharply.

"Oh-*ho!*" Sandy said.

"*Olé!*" David said.

"*Ai toro!*" Aníbal said, and picked up his napkin and waved it flirtatiously at Rhoda.

"Let's order," I said. "I think we ought to order."

"Another drink, Annabelle?" David said.

"One more, but that is all," Aníbal said, and smiled at Rhoda, and put the napkin back on his lap.

"Another scotch and water, miss," David said to the waitress.

Aníbal was ossified by the time we got around to ordering. He told us all about a cousin of his who was a prostitute, and about another cousin who had been war counselor of a gang on 112th Street before he'd been busted by the cops, and who was now serving five years at Sing Sing, and he told us how he himself had once been picked up for carrying a knife, and of how he had got off with a suspended sentence even though he was eighteen at the time and could no longer be considered a juvenile offender. He told us he had seen *West Side Story* and rooted for the Puerto Ricans, but that his wish was to become a real American (like you, Rosa), which is why he had, when filling out the questionnaire, specifically asked for an *American* girl, and was somewhat surprised when they had supplied a girl who was of Chinese and Jewish ancestry, though of course Jewish *is* American, who is the Chinese, he asked, your mother or your father?

"Her grandfather was Chinese," Sandy said.

My grandfather was a Spaniard, Aníbal said proudly, who owned seventy acres of land and a farm in the *Meseta,* as well as a town house in Salamanca, a very wealthy man. He had gone to Puerto Rico to visit his brother in April of 1936, only to receive word from home some three months later that the country was fast approaching civil war, and he had best hurry home to protect his interests. Aníbal seemed somewhat vague as to whether or not his grandfather had hurried home (he was, in fact, rather vague about *everything* along about then), but in any event it seemed the land was seized by the government, along with the town house (which sounded very fishy to me;

I didn't think Franco had behaved that way), and
grandfather had emigrated to Puerto Rico with his
family, a broken man who was now poor but still honest. (It occurred to me, while Aníbal was telling his
story, that I had never met a poor person who did not
claim his ancestors had been wealthy and powerful.)
Old grandfather apparently did not fare too well in
Puerto Rico, and died still poor but honest (not to
mention proud) in the shack on the edge of the sea,
his legacy to his only son, Luis, who was Aníbal's father. So now, here in this wonderful land of opportunity, Aníbal was ready to restore honor and wealth to the
family name by becoming an accountant and eventually
buying his own home in, as he put it, "a nice residential
section of the Bronx."

"That's very nice up there in the Bronx," Sandy
said.

"Almost like country," David said, and winked at
me.

"*Sí, sí,* I know," Aníbal said.

We had begun eating by then, and some of the alcohol effect was beginning to wear off, but he was still
slurring his words, and swaying gently in his seat, and
smiling beatifically at Rhoda, who was furious at us for
what we'd done, and even more furious at Aníbal for
having allowed it to happen. When Aníbal ordered a
brandy after the meal (Sandra, you will join me now?
he asked, and Sandy shook her head demurely and answered, Oh, thank you, Annabelle, I don't think so)
Rhoda became nearly apoplectic. Aníbal finally staggered out into the street with us at about a quarter past
ten, having paid the lion's share of the check, which
was only fair since he'd drunk so much.

The town was its usual Saturday-night self, riotously
asleep even here in the business district. We crossed
the street to avail ourselves of the big weekend enter-
tainment—Woolworth's lighted window—and then
headed down for the bay front and the parking lot

where Aníbal had left his car. The lampposts threw spaced circles of light into the blackness. Aníbal reeled along beside us, throwing his arms wide and bursting into song whenever he stepped into one of the circles, like a performer in successive spotlights. We were perhaps three or four blocks from the parking lot—were, in fact, crossing the street to get on the same side as the lot—when we saw them.

I'm not sure they would have recognized us if our reaction hadn't been so immediate and so obvious. But the three of us froze at once, stopping stock-still in the middle of the street as Rhoda and Aníbal moved forward to the sidewalk and then turned to see what was delaying us. The three boys were dressed just as they'd been dressed on the night of The Big Rape Scene, almost as though having once been typecast they refused to accept any other roles, levis, tee shirts, wide belts, loafers. They swaggered up the sidewalk, pushing each other and laughing, and then saw us, stopping the moment we did, freezing in an attitude of uncertainty. Then one of them let out a yell that chilled me to the marrow, "It's *Long* Legs!" he shouted, his voice rising, the simple exclamation loaded with something more than merely joy of recognition, shrill with discovery, thoroughly malevolent in its promise of revenge for the merry chase we'd led them and the razzing we'd administered from the deck of the ferry.

I was terrified this time.

This time the danger was unmistakable, there was no wondering about illusion this time, there was only panic being pounded into the heart like a splintery wooden stake. What happened next happened in split-second sequence, and yet it all seemed to overlap, the only concession reality made to distortion. I grabbed Sandy's hand and started to run, and then I head David's voice shouting, "Run!" and then I remembered Rhoda, and dropped Sandy's hand, and whirled, and stopped, and Sandy shouted, "Come *on,* for Christ's sake!" and I ran to the curb as the three boys raced down the sidewalk, and saw the angry face of one of them, and seized Rhoda's hand, and heard David yell "Let's get *out* of here!" and Rhoda said "What?" and idiotically I thought of the three astronauts who had been trapped inside the Apollo rocket when the flash fire erupted, and the way one of them in his last few seconds alive had shrieked in what the *Times* described as a shrill voice, "Get us out of here!" I caught another fast glimpse of the boy's face as he approached, and then saw that Aníbal had his mouth open, and I lunged forward and pulled Rhoda off the sidewalk, and heard Sandy shout, "Stop them, Annabelle! They're after Rhoda!"

Aníbal reacted at once. He planted his feet wide, clenched his fists and calmly and deliberately and drunkenly waited for the rush of the first boy, who was almost upon him now. This was something he understood, Sandy had chosen precisely the words to hurl at him, "They're after Rhoda!" This was pride and this was honor and this was manhood, and this was only the code that had contributed to the flow of *mucho sangre* along 111th Street and environs, "They're after our girl, they're after our turf, they're after our balls, get them, get them, get them!" I suddenly wondered if he'd told us even one tenth of the truth about his life in Spanish Harlem, and as we ran across the street again, I turned for a last look at Aníbal Gomez. Hunched forward in the light of the lamppost, wearing his neat brown suit, swaying somewhat with the liquor that still fumed inside him, he stood with his slender accountant's hands clenched, and bravely prepared to defend the honor of the wrong girl the computer had provided.

"God*damn* you, come *on!*" Sandy shouted, and the hero Aníbal Gomez burned himself in my mind in brown silhouette, and I thought again of the heroes in the space capsule and the way they had been reduced to merely terrified human beings at the end, and wondered if Aníbal Gomez would also scream to the unseen power that was NASA Control or whoever when three townie hoods tried to stomp out his brains—but it was Rhoda who screamed instead and tried to go back to him.

I grabbed her hand, I swung her around, I pulled her up the street. She was still screaming. Sandy ran over to where we were struggling. Behind us, I could hear grunting sounds, the muffled thud of fists, gentle mayhem, while here apart from the danger Rhoda screamed to the night and Sandy approached with terror-filled blue eyes, blond hair streaming from beneath the red wig, and quickly brought her hand to Rhoda's mouth to smother the cries. I grabbed Rhoda's arms and held them pinned to her sides while she squirmed and struggled to get loose, trying to calm her, knowing her screams would do no good, we did not want police on the scene, we did not want to have to explain fuzz to our parents. She was wearing lipstick Sandy had expertly helped her to apply, her mouth was slippery, she twisted her head sharply to the left leaving a wide blood-red smear on the right side of her face, escaping Sandy's hand and screaming again, screaming hysterically while behind us the grunting went on, the pulpy sound of fists, the soft noise of people sweating hard to kill each other. "Hold her!" Sandy shouted, grasping for her mouth again—and Rhoda bit her.

She yanked back her hand. A look of startled rage crossed her face. "You fucking idiot!" she shrieked, and reached for her again, lips skinned back, teeth bared as if to return the bite. Something slid into her eyes. Intelligence or guile, cunning or concern, it jarred her to an immediate stop. Trembling, she forced a smile onto her mouth and gently said, "Rhoda, we can't stay here. Come on, Rhoda. Please."

Rhoda nodded.

We began running toward the ferry slip.

Behind us, I heard Aníbal scream, *"Ayúdeme, por Dios, ayúdeme!"*

The night wasn't over yet, the night was just beginning.

Rhoda wept all the way back to the island, sitting inside on the ferry, and attracting the attention of several grownups who must have thought Christ knew what. We tried to calm her down, but she just kept shaking her head and weeping, so finally the three of us went outside and stood on the deck, but we didn't say anything to each other, we just kept watching the water slide by the boat.

I felt lousy.

When we got to Greensward, we took a jitney up the beach and said goodnight to each other without making any plans for the next day. I went inside the house and could tell immediately that it was empty. This was Saturday night, and the end-of-August parties had already started, a week sooner than they should have. My parents were certain to be out having a grand old time, Daddy guzzling scotch and Mommy shooting green-eyed daggers at him. I went into my room, took off my clothes, put on a nightshirt I had bought from a guy who went to boarding school, and climbed into bed. I kept thinking of Aníbal Gomez facing those hoods. I kept hearing the soft sounds of combat.

I was walking through a castle. Alfred Hitchcock was showing me through the castle. There were large high stone rooms. There were tattered drapes hanging at arched windows. There was a closed door. "Don't go into that room," Hitchcock warned me. The door of the room opened a crack. Sandy in her mother's red wig whispered, "Come to me, Peter, come see my tits." David was behind her, grinning. His hands came up. He began fondling her nipples. The door closed. "Don't go into that room," Hitchcock said again.

The castle was endless.

I tried to follow Hitchcock, but he was walking very fast, and I lost him. I was alone in what must have been the ballroom, with a huge chandelier hanging in the center of it, candles guttering, torn drapes moving at the windows, dust on the floor, knee-deep dust that rose and settled as I walked through it.

The candles went out.

There were things in the darkness, bats or birds. They flew silently about my head. I could hear the soft flutter of their wings. The dust was deeper. I had difficulty moving through it. It was higher on my body, it had risen to my chest.

"That is the dust of corpses," Hitchcock's voice said.

The fluttering above my head stopped. There was stillness. The dust had risen to my neck. I pushed through it in panic. I had to get back to the room. The dust touched my nostrils. I began breathing it. It was in my mouth and in my nose. I tried to push it away from my face. I saw the closed door through the darkness, through the dust. The dust was heavy and thick, I pushed through it and breathed it and spit it and choked on it. I reached the door. I forced my hand through the dust and clutched the doorknob. "Come," Sandy said. "Hurry," David said. I could not turn the knob. I struggled with the knob. The dust was rising over my head. I was suffocating. *"Ayúdeme,"* I shouted, *"por Dios, ayúdeme!"* and the knob turned, and the door opened.

The room was white, white walls, white ceiling, white floor, white drapes flowing over windows through which a blinding white light streamed.

They were moaning.

They were in the far corner of the room where the white walls joined, naked and white on the white polished floor, fucking.

I screamed.

"Peter," the voice said.

I screamed again.

"Oh, Peter," the voice said.

I opened my eyes.

My father was sitting by the side of the bed.

"Oh, Peter," he said, "oh, Peter."

"Get away from me!" I screamed.

"Oh, Peter," he said, "oh, Peter."

I got out of bed. I was sweating. I ran out of the bedroom, and then out of the house, and I stood outside breathing hard and saw the light in my father's bedroom go on. I heard my mother say something in an angry voice, and heard an object falling, and my father cursing, and then the light went out and everything was still. I kept watching the house for a long time.

When I finally went inside, my father was snoring. I tiptoed over to the open bedroom door and looked in. My mother was asleep, too. I went into the living room.

I opened a fifth of Cutty Sark and took it with me into my bedroom. I drank right from the bottle. I must have finished half the bottle, and then I guess I passed out.

I slept until eleven.

It was a bright hot muggy day. The sheets were sticking to me when I woke up, and I was covered with sweat. I felt mean and hot and surly. I looked at the clock on the dresser, and then I called David while I was still in bed and asked him what the plan was for the day.

"You know what the plan is," he said.

"What do you mean?"

"You know," he said.

"I don't think I can get the boat," I said. "This is Sunday. My father'll probably want to use it again."

"Oh," David said. "Yeah."

"So it'll have to wait till tomorrow," I said.

"Yeah," David said, and sighed. "Well, I'll give Sandy a ring, we'll probably go out to the point."

"Okay," I said, and hesitated. "You think I should call Rhoda?"

"Why not?"

"Well, she seemed pretty upset last night."

"She's probably fine by now," David said. "You going to stop by here for me?"

"Yeah, sure, give me a half hour, okay?"

"Right, I'll call Sandy."

"And you think I should call Rhoda, huh?"

"Sure," David said, and hung up.

I put the phone back on the cradle and looked up at the ceiling. There were four squashed mosquitoes near the light fixture in the center of the room. I had killed them at the very beginning of the summer, before my father and I had put up the screens. I thought of the night before, and then sighed and got out of bed. I didn't feel like calling Rhoda just yet. I felt that if I called her right then, I would probably begin yelling at her over the phone, that was the way I felt. I had a terrible headache and I was a little sick to my stomach. I had never drunk hard liquor before, and I decided now that I didn't like it at all, not if it made you feel this way afterward. I sneaked the half-empty fifth back into the living room, and then I went into the kitchen and told my mother I'd like some orange juice and cold cereal, but nothing else. She naturally raised a fuss, so I also had scrambled eggs and corn muffins and then vomited everything up in the bathroom.

I was getting dressed for the beach when the telephone rang. It was Sandy, and she sounded very cheerful.

"Hello, gorgeous," she said, "how do you feel this morning?"

"Just great," I said, and pulled a face.

"I wonder how Annabelle made out," she said.

"I don't know."

"He shouldn't have got so drunk."

"Well . . ."

"I called Rhoda," she said, changing the subject. "We want to go out to the point, is that okay with you?"

"Sure." I hesitated and then said, *"You* called Rhoda?"

"Sure. Why not?"

"Well, last night . . ."

"Oh, she was hysterical last night," Sandy said. "You can't blame her, can you? I was pretty scared myself."

"So was I."

"That was cool," Sandy said. "What Annabelle did."

"Mmm."

"But he should have known better than to drink so much."

"I guess so," I said.

"Okay, we'll meet you out at the point in ten minutes or so, okay?"

"Yes," I said, "fine."

"It's very hot," Sandy said, and hung up.

"Where are you going?" my mother asked.

"Out to the point."

"The water's supposed to be rough today," she said. "Be careful."

"We're always careful," I said.

"Ha-ha," my mother said.

My father came out of the bedroom in his bathrobe. "Good morning, son," he said.

"Will you be using the boat today?" I asked.

"I don't know. Ellie?" he said, turning to my mother.

"We promised the Conlons," my mother said, "but what do you think? The water's supposed to be rough today."

"There aren't any warnings up, are there?"

"No, but the water's supposed to be rough."

"Well, let's give it a try. We promised the Conlons."

"All right," my mother said.

"Sorry, son," my father said.

"That's okay," I said. "So that's where we'll be, out at the point."

"Be careful," my mother said again, and I left the house.

The beach was suffocatingly hot and thronged with people. This was Sunday and the normal weekday crowd should have been doubled or at most trebled, but the incredible heat had driven the entire world to the shore, and people sprawled now on every available inch of sand, hoping for a vagrant breeze. There was no wind at all, but the ocean was rough nonetheless, with huge waves rolling in and breaking furiously against the shore. The sky was a yellowish white, not a trace of blue anywhere, not a single cloud breaking the glaring oval that stretched like wet skin over ocean and beach. It was difficult to breathe. The sun seemed to be everywhere and nowhere, the air shimmered with diffused light. I remembered that I'd left my sunglasses back at the house, but the sand was too hot to make a return trip even thinkable. By the time I reached David's house, I was exhausted. He was waiting for me on the sundeck.

"Hot, huh, Poo?" he said.

I nodded.

"How'd you like that Annabelle?" he said.

"Yeah."

"He shouldn't have got so drunk. You ready to go?"

"Yeah," I said, "let's go."

We started walking up the beach. It was hard hot work. We were silent for a long time.

"It doesn't seem real," I said at last.

"What doesn't?"

"Last night. Annabelle."

"It *wasn't* real," David said, and laughed. "The computer dreamed it up."

"I just hope he didn't get in any trouble."

"What do you mean?"

"With the police or anything?"

"Oh, I'm sure he didn't," David said.

"How do you know?"

"Well, I don't."

"Yeah, that's just it," I said.

"He shouldn't have drunk so much," David said. "There they are."

They had spread a blanket near the water's edge; they both looked up as we approached, but only Sandy waved.

"Damn it, I forgot the umbrella," David said.

"Oh, great."

"Why didn't you remind me?"

"Where's the umbrella?" Sandy said immediately.

"He forgot it," I said.

"We'll roast. It's like the Sahara out here."

"Let's get in the water."

"I'm for that."

"Not me," Rhoda said.

"Hi," I said.

"Hi," she said, but she did not smile.

"It's not as rough as it looks," Sandy said. "Once you get past the breakers . . ."

"No, not me," Rhoda said.

"Okay," Sandy said, and without another word got up and went into the water. David followed her. I sat on the blanket beside Rhoda. Her face was all squinched up against the glare, and her eyes were red and puffy from the crying she'd done the night before. There were blankets and umbrellas everywhere around us, transistor radios going, girls spreading suntan oil on their bellies and legs, kids throwing balls, kids filling pails and dumping them to make sand cakes, guys doing headstands, couples necking.

"I've never seen it this crowded," I said.

"It's the day," Rhoda said. "It's so hot."

"It's like Coney Island, for Christ's sake."

Rhoda nodded. Sandy and David plunged through a rolling breaker, disappeared from sight, surfaced some five feet beyond and began swimming toward the deeper water. I watched them. The light glaring from the water was intense. I shielded my eyes with one hand, and then was suddenly aware that Rhoda was staring at me. I turned to look at her. Her face was still closed tight against the sun.

"I'm sorry about last night," I said.

She nodded, but did not answer.

"Rhoda, I'm sorry. I'm really very sorry."

"Peter," she said, "why did you get him drunk?"

"I don't know," I said.

"I asked you to stop . . ."

"I know you did."

". . . I begged you to stop."

"I can't explain it, I really can't."

"Peter," she said, "do you know that I love you?"

"I . . . I guess I know it," I said. I was suddenly frightened. All at once, I wanted to get off that blanket and shove my way through the teeming noisy humanity everywhere around us, and splash into the water to where Sandy and David were swimming. I did not want to hear anything else Rhoda had to say. I had the feeling that whatever else she said from this point on would be painful, more painful than the nightmare had been, more painful than the headache, more painful than throwing up in the toilet. I wanted her to stop at once, to leave things exactly where they stood, accept my apology graciously, and merely shut the hell up.

Tilting her head to one side, squinting at me, she began pounding me with words instead, her mouth in constant motion, the metal bands blinking accompanying semaphore as they intermittently caught sunlight. A bead of perspiration slid from my armpit to my ribs, trailed across my chest and ran down over my abdomen. Rhoda's voice rose and fell, and with it the sounds of the beach, reverberating on the air, muffled, indistinct. There was laughter in counterpoint, sporadic laughter that seemed continuous even though it came from separate sources at different times. The ocean roared, but seemed curiously overwhelmed by the hovering buzz and the laughter and Rhoda's insistent voice. I felt suddenly apart, as though I had been paralyzed in mid-motion and then gilded with sunshine while everyone around me continued to move and breathe and sweat and make noise. Rhoda's lips were still in action, her bands blinking. I sat still and silent on the blanket at the water's edge, a stunned nucleus at the center of incessant turmoil.

She had lain awake all night trying to understand my behavior, she said. She loved me so much, she said, and that was why she couldn't understand. I had been so gentle in the forest that day, so sweet and loving and gentle, and yet last night I seemed to join the others in their malicious conspiracy to intoxicate Aníbal. What *was* it between the three of us, what was the secret that seemed to generate such unanimous enthusiasm for the unerringly wrong idea? It had been wrong to go out with Aníbal to begin with, she should never have allowed us to talk her into it, but when the three of us got together that way, we made all the *right* things seem shameful and square. Oh, Peter, she said, I don't *want* to be square, I want so much to understand you, but what can I think when you deliberately conspire to get a poor man drunk? Did you do it for fun, did you enjoy watching him make a fool of himself, the way you watched those poor unfortunate perverts that day (Lower your voice, I warned) on Violet's island, why did you do it, Peter? Peter, was it square to find something appealing in Aníbal Gomez, to want to hear him out even when he went on and on about his grandfather, so terribly square to want to grant him the respect of listening? (I don't need this, Rhoda, I thought, I don't need you for a conscience!)

So why did you do it, that's what I'm trying to understand? You knew I didn't want you to, I tried to stop you often enough, I *pleaded* with you to stop, and yet you went right ahead with it, getting him so drunk he didn't know what he was doing, and then pitting him against those three hoodlums, who *were* those three boys, anyway?

"Some boys," I said.

"Who?"

"Just some boys."

Peter, she said, this is just what frightens me, this is just what I was trying to tell you about, this loss of feeling for anything that's *real*. Aníbal was *real*, Peter, he was a very real person, and you got him drunk just for kicks, and then threw him up against those boys without a thought, almost as if he were made of plastic. Peter, we're *not* made of plastic yet, we don't have plastic hearts and livers and lungs, we don't run around on plastic wheels, we don't have plastic tapes inside us telling us what to love or hate, not yet we don't.

"Nobody said we did," I answered.

"Peter, don't I matter to you at all?" she asked.

"Rhoda," I said, "I don't know if you realize how serious the situation was last night."

"You didn't answer my question," she said.

"Those guys weren't fooling around," I said. "If they'd have caught us . . ."

"Then why didn't *you* try to stop them? Why'd you send Annabelle?"

"I didn't send anybody."

"Sandy did. She sent a skinny little . . ."

"He wasn't skinny."

"He *was* skinny, and he was drunk."

"Well, he shouldn't have got drunk," I said, and sighed and looked out over the water. I felt intimately but mistakenly involved with her, as though everyone around us wrongly assumed we'd been whispering lovers' secrets to each other, as though even our silence now blatantly advertised a relationship that didn't really exist. I had not asked her to love me. I had not even asked her to understand me. I felt suddenly trapped. Anxiously, I searched the water, looking beyond the crashing surf to the choppy waves hoping that David and Sandy would come out to join me. I thought again that I should get up and leave Rhoda, plunge into the ocean, let the cold water shock me back to life, wash off the sunshine gilt that was paralyzing me. I didn't want her to start crying again, though; I couldn't bear the thought of her crying again. At the same time, I didn't want anymore of *this* crap, either.

"Listen," I said, "I don't find this conversation very pleasant."

"Neither do I."

"So let's talk about something else."

"No, let's talk about what you did last night."

"Oh, Rhoda, for Christ's sake, get *off* it!" I had raised my voice, and I turned swiftly now to see if I'd attracted anyone's attention. The couple on the next blanket were soul-kissing. A tidal wave could have moved in from Hawaii to inundate California, the Middle Western states and the entire Eastern seaboard without disturbing them. I looked back at Rhoda and whispered, "What the hell did I do that was so awful, would you mind telling me?"

"You behaved like a coward," she said.

"Oh, thanks."

"You ran."

"That doesn't make me a coward."

"Doesn't it?"

"I didn't want my skull bashed in. Also, Rhoda, I came *back* for you. Perhaps you've forgotten that I came back for you."

"No, I haven't forgotten that. Why'd you come back, Peter?"

"Because you were in danger."

"Then why didn't you stay and help Annabelle?"

"Because Annabelle means nothing to me."

"Do *I*?"

"I don't know, Rhoda."

"All right," she said.

"And that's the truth."

"All right," she said again.

"Rhoda," I said, "let's get this straight, okay?"

"Okay," she said.

"You're a swell person," I said, "and I really like you."

"Thank you."

"And most of the time, I enjoy being with you. That day in the forest, for example, when we were talking, I felt . . . Rhoda, I felt almost happier than I've ever felt in my life. I hope you believe me, Rhoda."

"I believe you, Peter."

"And I find you very attractive, too, and sexy, well, I really shouldn't talk this way."

"I don't mind, Peter."

"But Rhoda, when you start *analyzing* everything . . ."

"I'm sorry, Peter."

"It's just that you make me feel awful."

"I'm sorry. Really I am."

"You see, Rhoda . . ."

"Yes, Peter?"

"We didn't mean any harm last night."

She stared at me silently for a long while. Her eyes were wide and serious, challenging the sun's glare, challenging my face, challenging my words. She suddenly looked old. I had once seen a photograph of an Oklahoma sharecropper, a woman with suffering silence in her eyes, pain drawing her mouth tight, weariness etched into every line of her face. Rhoda looked just that way now.

"Didn't you?" she said at last. "Didn't you mean any harm?"

"We were only trying to have a little fun," I said.

"A little fun," she repeated blankly.

"We didn't know the night was going to turn out the way it did. Rhoda, we *couldn't* have known."

"No, you couldn't have known," she said.

"Rhoda, for Christ's sake, don't start *in* again. You make me feel . . ."

"I'm sorry."

"Yes, you're sorry, but you keep *doing* it all the time. Why can't you just . . . ?"

"Just *what*, Peter?"

"Just . . . just shut up every now and then?"

"Not speak?" she said. "Not think?" she said.

"Oh, Jesus," I said.

"I didn't want to come here today," she said, "I *knew* I shouldn't have come."

"Then why the hell *did* you?"

"Because Sandy was so sweet on the phone, and I thought . . ."

"Sandy doesn't bear grudges," I said.

"Must you *always* side with her?"

"You shouldn't have bit her."

"She shouldn't have sent Annabelle to fight those . . ."

"Are we back to that again?"

"Yes, we'll *always* be back to that again!"

"Rhoda," I said, "you're beginning to give me a fat pain in the ass." I rose suddenly, brushed sand from my thighs, and said, "I'm going in."

"Peter . . ."

"Yes?" I had my hands on my hips, and I was looking down at her.

"Nothing," she said.

"I thought maybe you wanted to come in," I said, and grinned.

"No. I'm afraid."

"You're afraid of too many things," I said. "That's your trouble." I looked down at her a moment longer, and then turned and walked to the water's edge and plunged through the crashing surf. The ocean was cold and dark. I swam underwater for perhaps fifteen feet with my eyes wide open, but I couldn't see a thing. When I surfaced, I opened my mouth to gulp in some air, and a high choppy wave hit me full in the face. Coughing, I treaded water, and looked around for David and Sandy, spotting them farther out. I swam over to them.

"Hi," Sandy said.

"Hi, beautiful."

"Nice lovely calm day, isn't it?" David said.

"Oh, delightful," I said.

"I'm bare-assed," Sandy said.

"Really?"

"Look," she said, and held up her bikini pants.

"What's the difference between America and France?" David asked.

"I don't know," I said, the perfect straight man. "What's the difference between America and France?"

"In America," David said, "your goose is cooked, but in France," he said, "your cook is goosed," and suddenly Sandy let out a surprised yell and leaped about three feet out of the water. I couldn't imagine what it was at first; the only thing I could think of was a shark. And then I realized that David had goosed her, and I burst out laughing.

"You sneaky bastard," Sandy said, laughing, and swam over to him with her sopping wet pants in one hand, and then hit him on the head with them, and tried to duck him. I went to his rescue and the three of us wrestled around out there for maybe five minutes, laughing and yelling, and then Sandy put on her pants, and we floated on our backs for I guess another fifteen minutes or so.

By two o'clock the heat was intolerable.

"You're going to die, Rhoda," Sandy said, "unless you get in the water."

"I'm afraid of it today," Rhoda said.

"If you want to go in . . ."

"No."

". . . we'll stay with you. We won't let her drown, will we?"

"Certainly not," David said.

"I'm all right," Rhoda said. "I don't mind the heat."

"You're sweating like a pig," David said.

"Ladies don't sweat, they glow," Sandy said.

"What the hell does that mean?"

"It's a line from a play we did last term."

"It sounds like a great play."

"It was a very good play, as a matter of fact."

"Did anybody bring sandwiches?"

"Rhoda, where are those sandwiches you made?"

"I'm not hungry yet," I said.

"It's too hot to eat, anyway," Rhoda said.

"Why don't we get off the beach?" Sandy suggested. "Go have a picnic lunch someplace."

"Where?" David asked.

"The forest," Sandy answered.

"What forest?" Rhoda said.

"Where the fire was."

There was very little motion on the beach. The sun had robbed everyone of the will to move, the sun had fused bodies to blankets. Conversation had stopped, there was scarcely any laughter. An unfamiliar silence shimmered on the air like heat itself, broken only by the incessant rumble of the surf and the droning of the sand flies. The flies were everywhere. They circled the head and landed on the neck and shoulders. They

crawled over bellies and legs, stinging, elusively taking
wing whenever you slapped at them.

"This is impossible," Sandy said. "What do you
say?"

"Where's the forest?" Rhoda asked.

"The center of the island."

"Is it nice?"

"It's horrible," I said.

"It'll be cooler than here," David said.

"It'll be private," Sandy said.

"Rhoda?"

"No," she said, "I don't think so."

"Well, it's no damn good *here*," Sandy said. "Come
on, Rhoda."

"I don't mind the heat."

"Look at the sweat pouring off you."

"In China . . ." Rhoda started.

"If you won't go in the water . . ."

". . . they drink hot tea in order to sweat, and then
they sit in the shade of a tree, and the sweat evapo-
rates, and they feel cool all over."

"This isn't China," David said, "and there aren't
any trees on the beach."

"And I'm sweating enough without any tea," Sandy
said.

"Come on, Rhoda."

"No," Rhoda said, "I like it here."

"Rhoda, you can be pretty goddamn obstinate, you
know that?" Sandy said.

"I'm sorry."

"I can stop off for some beer," David said, and
shrugged.

"Come on, Rhoda."

"No."

"Okay, we'll go without you." Sandy got off the
blanket. Her pants were still damp and sand was clinging to them. She brushed the sand off with swift flat

palm strokes. Then she adjusted her top, and said, "Are you coming, Peter?"

"That forest gives me the creeps," I said.

"It'll be cool."

"I'll sneak out some beer," David said.

"If your parents . . ."

"That's all blown over."

"Come on," Sandy said.

"Well . . ." I said.

"Oh, look, it's too hot to argue," she said, and picked up her beach bag, slung it over her shoulder, and began threading her way through the sprawled bodies, heading for the dune.

"Poo, you are making a big mistake," David said. He took his towel in both hands, and snapped it like a whip at a sand fly on the blanket, missing. He shrugged philosophically, and then started off after Sandy.

"It *is* pretty hot," I said.

"You can go if you want to," Rhoda said.

"Well . . ."

"Go on. If you want to."

"Will you be all right?" I asked.

She nodded.

"Are you sure?"

She nodded again.

"I think I ought to," I said. I turned away from her gaze. "It's so hot here," I said.

"Yes, go," she said.

I picked up my sneakers. "You sure you'll be okay?"

"Yes," she said, and again nodded.

"Okay then," I said. "Hey, wait up!" I yelled to David, and ran after him.

We walked single file on the narrow boardwalk, Sandy in the lead with her beach bag hitting against her thigh, David with his towel slung around his neck, me trying to keep up while struggling to get my sneak-

ers on. David began humming one of his symphonies.
When we got to his house, he went inside and I sat
down on the porch steps to tie my sneakers. Sandy was
on the railing, looking off toward the beach. Her long
hair hung limply, sticking in spidery tendrils to her
cheeks. She raised her hand idly and wiped sweat from
between her breasts, and then left her hand under the
bra, as though trying to feel her heartbeat.

"Jesus, it's hot," she said.

I stood up and bounced a bit in my sneakers. "What
do you suppose it is?" I asked.

"Ninety-eight, I'll bet."

"More like a hundred."

"Rhoda's an idiot," Sandy said.

"She's okay," I said.

I sat on the steps again. Everything was so still.
Sandy began jiggling her foot. Inside the house, we
heard Eudice say something, and then David's voice
answering. Sandy raised her eyebrows. We both listened, but the house was silent again. In a little while,
David came out with his poncho. He winked at us and
started down the steps. We followed immediately.

"Trouble?" I asked.

"Nope."

"Have you got it?" Sandy said.

"Yep. Six bottles."

"Two each," Sandy said, and grinned. "Good." She
gave her beach bag a little twirl, slung it over her
shoulder again, and began walking. David fell into step
beside me.

"Know what else I've got?" he whispered.

"What?" I whispered back.

"Guess," he said, and winked.

"Oh."

"Mmm," he said, and that was when we heard Rhoda's voice behind us.

"Peter!" she called. "Peter, wait for me!"

"Oh, shit," David said.

Sandy turned. "Well, well," she said, "it's Rhoda."

We waited for her on the path. She was carrying the blanket and a large brown paper bag. She was out of breath when she reached us. Panting, she said, "You forgot the sandwiches."

"We thought we'd lost you," Sandy said, and smiled.

"May I still come along?"

"Get too hot for you on the beach?" David asked sourly.

"I changed my mind," Rhoda said.

"Come," Sandy said.

We began walking. I took the sandwiches from Rhoda. David looked back at me with a disgruntled expression on his face. We walked in silence, the beach bag hanging from Sandy's shoulder, thudding against her thigh with every step she took. The sun was hot. We were climbing up and away from the beach. The sound of the ocean was very far behind us now. We continued to climb. I suddenly wished that Rhoda had not joined us.

I wasn't sure why I felt that way exactly. I only know that as we got closer to the forest, as I saw the burnt trees in a shimmering haze ahead of me and above me, I remembered that once there had been a fire here, remembered that this was where Sandy had killed the gull, this was where David and I had pounded him to a pulp. And then I remembered sitting with Sandy behind the huge black boulder, and I thought of what David had picked up at the house, and of what we might have done to Sandy if Rhoda hadn't suddenly decided to join us. That wasn't exactly it, though. That wasn't all of it. I don't know what it was. I was frightened. I wanted to tell Rhoda not to go into the forest, the way Hitchcock had warned me not to go into the room. I wanted to tell Rhoda to get the hell back to the beach.

The burnt pines were gnarled and black against the sky.

"Are you all right?" I asked Rhoda.

"Yes, I'm fine," she said.

"Do you want me to carry that blanket?"

"No, I can manage."

We found the huge boulder, as black as the skeletal trees surrounding it. Sandy went to it unerringly and kicked aside some bleached and rodent-picked bones that might have been the gull's, I don't know. We spread the poncho on the ground. I sat with my back against the boulder, and Rhoda sat beside me. I was trembling. David opened four bottles of beer.

"No, I don't want any," Rhoda said.

"Take one," Sandy said. There was a sudden flick of harshness in her voice.

"All . . . all right," Rhoda said.

David handed her an open bottle, and then sat on the poncho with us. Sandy was still standing. She accepted the bottle of beer David offered to her, tilted it to her mouth, said, *"Skoal,"* and drank. "Mmm, that's good," she said. "Isn't it good, Rhoda?"

"It's just that it's so bitter," Rhoda said.

"Got to take the bitter with the sweet, baby," David said, and laughed. He drank, belched, said, "Beg your pardon," and drank some more.

"It's just as hot here as it was on the beach," Sandy said.

"Not a breeze," David said.

"Why don't we go?" I said, and started to get up.

"After all that climbing?" Sandy said. "Sit down, Peter."

I eased myself back against the boulder. Sandy finished her beer and threw the bottle into the bushes.

"Another one?" David asked.

"Why not?" she said.

"Isn't anybody hungry?" Rhoda asked.

"I'm famished, baby," David said, and laughed again. There was an odd sound to his laughter. He seemed very nervous. He belched again, drained his

bottle, and tried to throw it into the bushes where
Sandy had thrown hers. But the bottle hit the branch
of a burnt tree, and the branch broke off and fell to
the forest floor. A cloud of black dust rose on the air.
The sound of the crackling branch echoed and then
died. David handed Sandy another open bottle.

"*Skoal,*" she said.

"*Skoal,*" David said, and again laughed the same
nervous laugh.

"You're not drinking, Rhoda."

"I really don't like the taste of it," Rhoda said, and
put her bottle down.

*Good,* I thought.

"It won't go to waste," Sandy said, and shrugged.

"We'll share it," David said.

"Share and share alike, right," Sandy said, and giggled. "Right, Peter?"

"What?"

"Share and share alike, right?"

"Oh," I said, "yes."

"Wouldn't anyone like a sandwich?" Rhoda asked,
and reached into the brown paper bag.

"Don't knock over that beer, honey," David said.

"Oh, I'm sorry, I . . ."

"Here, let me have that," Sandy said. She lifted
Rhoda's bottle, and then, holding a bottle in either
hand, drank a little from each one and said, "Major
truth: it is very hot in this goddamn forest. Remember
that day, Peter? Remember the truth serum?"

"Yes," I said, and glanced at Rhoda.

"Hey, you said we would *share* it," David said, and
got up and walked to where Sandy was standing. She
handed him the bottle. He drained it and threw it into
the bushes.

"There's ham," Rhoda said, "and there's also roast
beef. What would you like, Peter?"

"Peter would like to finish his beer," Sandy said.

"I thought . . ."

"Wouldn't you, Peter?"

"Well, I can eat at the same time," I said, and shrugged. "I'll have a ham sandwich, Rhoda."

"Rhoda made those sandwiches with her own little hands," Sandy said. "Didn't you, Rhoda?"

"Yes. Yes, I did."

"Going to make someone a great little wife," David said, and sat down again.

"Can you sew, Rhoda?"

"Well, not really too well."

"She can't sew, David."

"Pity. I guess she *won't* make someone a great little wife."

I took the sandwich, bit into it, and washed it down with beer. "Doesn't anybody else want to eat?" I asked.

"I'll have something," Rhoda said, and reached into the bag again.

"I thought you said it was too hot to eat," Sandy said.

"That was on the beach," Rhoda answered, and again I thought *Good,* and couldn't understand why I'd thought it, or even what I meant by it.

"And this is in the forest," Sandy said, "and it's hot as hell in the forest, too." She lifted the half-full bottle she was holding in her hand, and suddenly poured beer onto her breasts and into the front of her bikini top. "Ahhhhh," she said, "that's better," and tossed the empty bottle away. "But now my top is wet," she said, giggling. "Peter, my top is wet."

"Okay," I said.

"Don't you like girls who say things like My top is wet?"

"Yes, sure," I said.

"Don't you appreciate my honesty?"

"Sure I do."

"Why don't you take it off?" David suggested.

"Ho-ho," Sandy said, and rolled her eyes.

"Are we out of beer?" David asked.

"When you're out of beer," Sandy said, "you're out of beer."

"You can have what's left of this," I said. "I don't think I can finish it."

"What's the matter, Poo?" David said. "On the wagon?"

"No, I'm just not . . . thirsty," I said, and shrugged.

"Never mind," David said, "it won't go to waste."

"God, it's *hot!*" Sandy said.

David took the bottle, drank a little from it, and then handed it to Sandy. "Share and share alike," he said.

"Thank you," she said, and made a pretty little curtsy. She finished the beer, carefully put the empty bottle down on the ground, and took off the top of her suit.

Rhoda did not immediately see her. Her head was bent, she was chewing on her sandwich. She took the sandwich from her mouth and then tried to dislodge a piece of roast beef that had got caught in her bands, still not seeing Sandy, and then finally freeing the stubborn sliver of meat. She looked up. She caught her breath, and immediately turned away.

"What's the matter, Rhoda?" Sandy asked.

"Noth . . . nothing," she answered.

"Rhoda, you're going to choke on your sandwich," Sandy said, and giggled.

You mean she's going to swallow her braces," David said, laughing.

"I . . . I . . . Peter," she said, "I think I'd like to go now, please."

I sat stunned and uneasy and aware. I thought This is outrageous and then immediately realized I was only relating to Rhoda's shock and not to any belief of my own. This is *marvelous,* I thought, this is stimulating and daring, and was immediately overcome by fresh guilt when Rhoda plaintively touched my arm, but I could not take my eyes from Sandy. This is shameless, I thought, and the thought excited me, and I was thrilled and then embarrassed by my masculine response, and I thought I'd better get Rhoda out of here before something terrible happens, and then I began to anticipate what might happen, the way I'd anticipated getting Aníbal drunk, and stupidly I said, "Rhoda . . . fi . . . finish your sandwich."

"I'm not hungry," she said, and got up off the poncho.

Sandy stepped into her path.

"Where are you going?" she asked.

"Back . . . home. To the house. The house. Out of here. Out," she said.

"What's your hurry?" Sandy said. "Finish your sandwich. Peter wants you to finish your sandwich."

"No," she said. "Put your . . . cover yourself. Sandy, *cover* yourself."

"Why?"

"They can see."

"Who?"

"The boys."

"So what?"

"They can *see*."

"Yes," Sandy said.

David, who had been sitting quietly on the poncho, suddenly said, "Why don't you take *yours* off, Rhoda?"

"No!" she said sharply, and whirled toward him, and saw the smile on his face, and instantly stepped back and away from him. She almost collided with Sandy. Turning, she saw the identical smile on Sandy's face, and knew at once that she was trapped. Her hands fluttered up toward her breasts. She looked at me where I sat still and silent against the black rock.

"Peter," she said, "please."

"Do it," Sandy said.

"I couldn't. I can't. Peter, I can't. Peter . . ."

"Do it," David said.

"Please don't make me. Peter, please."

I took a deep breath. "Do it," I said.

Her eyes searched my face. She seemed about to say "Peter" again, her lips seemed pursed around my name, but nothing came from her mouth. She broke away suddenly instead, trying to step wide around Sandy, who grabbed her wrist and swung her back toward the poncho. "No, please," she said, and Sandy came swiftly toward her, hands outstretched, reaching for the bra top.

"Don't!" she shouted.

David came off the poncho, his fists clenched, a contorted look on his face, rose in one swift smooth sudden motion to seize Rhoda from behind while Sandy pulled the bra top down. Her breasts burst free, she tried to raise her hands to cover them, but David grabbed both her wrists and Sandy slapped her hard across the face, twice, the way she had slapped her that night we'd found her crying on the dune. She was not crying now. She fought wildly as they dragged her to the poncho, kicking. This isn't real, I thought, this isn't happening, trying to free her hands, I wanted to kiss her, I wanted to kiss her breasts, I wanted to hit her, David and Sandy grunting, the sounds muffled like the sounds on the mainland when Annabelle faced the hoods, I wanted to stop them, I wanted to laugh hysterically, "Oh, Peter," she said, "oh, Peter," I wanted to shout Leave her alone, can't you see? can't you see?, lips pulled back over metal bands, eyes wild and frightened, I wanted to save her and destroy her, trying to cover her breasts with her forearms, David forcing them away, I wanted to love her and protect her, I did not want involvement, I wanted to kiss her gently in the forest sunshine and listen to the sounds of life around us, I thought of Spotswood, New Jersey, and a clearing washed with yellow light, "Don't let them!"

she screamed, "Peter, don't *let* them!" and I remembered her column and what she had said about a *last* summer, hers and maybe everybody's, and I thought Are you trying to scare me, Rhoda? and *was* scared, and hated her, *I'm so afraid of winter coming,* and saw a confused tangle of bodies on the slippery poncho, unreal, moving too fast, Sandy's slender brown legs flashing, Rhoda's white and heavy breasts, David's arm muscles straining to keep her pinned, "I don't want to!" she screamed, and I thought You *have* to, "Stop them!" she screamed, and I thought *Them?* You mean *us,* don't you? You silly cautious girl, *this* is the party, *we're* the party, don't you know that? and felt an overwhelming sense of oneness with David, and found myself rolling over suddenly on the wet poncho, rolling toward Rhoda and her big white tits, moving together with David as if his body were my body, his muscles and hands were mine, Sandy falling suddenly against my back, taut and smooth and wet with sweat, kiss her, I thought, kiss Rhoda, and remembered for the last time that day on Violet's island and heard Sandy whisper, *"Get* her!"

We clutched for her breasts. "Leave me," she murmured, but we did not leave her, grabbed her breasts in rage instead, "Leave me, please," she mumbled, but we did not leave her, swept our hands in fury over her body, "Something," she said, "please," and together we stripped her naked. We pulled her pants down over her belly, "Please," she moaned, and her thighs, "Something," she whimpered, and her legs, "Something, something," she begged, and Sandy slapped her again, and she cowered on the sticky rubber poncho, shivering as we stood over her breathing harshly, our bodies covered with sweat, the forest silent and dead around us, Rhoda naked, her pants bunched stupidly around her ankles, naked, there was nothing we could not see. We reached for her pants together, pulled them over her feet, hurled them into the bushes. She tried to twist

away, tried to turn her body, raise her knees to hide
herself, but we shoved her flat to the poncho again,
and David said, "Hold her," and we held her. She
seemed dead. She lay on the poncho with her eyes
closed and her mouth tight, and I thought She's dead,
we've killed her.

He was taking off his trunks.

"Spread her," Sandy said.

She gave a final futile twist as we forced her legs
apart, trying to turn over on the poncho and away
from him as he walked to her, and stood above her,
and suddenly crouched, poised.

We did it to her.

He did it to her first, and then I did.

I was last.

As we walked out of the forest, Sandy said, "Is she
dressed yet?"

"Who?" David asked.

"Whatshername."

I turned to look over my shoulder.

She was standing by the round black rock, whimpering. She stooped crookedly to pull up her pants, and
then hunched her shoulders and dressed herself that
way, whimpering and hunched, flinching at every
crackling forest sound. She looked up only once, as
she fastened the top of her suit, and her eyes accident-
ally met mine, and then, quickly, she ducked her
head, and sidled away through the stunted bushes, her
head turned away from us, moved from us silhouetted
against the black trees in gnarled silhouette, the dead
distorted trees, not hurrying, moving with a slow broken crooked gait.

I watched her go.

"She's leaving," I said.

"Good," Sandy said.

"Do you think she'll tell?" David said.

"Not a chance," Sandy said, and smiled. "She's too scared."

"Why, that's right, she is," David said.

"Too scared of everything," I said.

We grinned. We all looked at each other and grinned. Then we began laughing. We must have laughed for about three or four minutes, our arms wrapped around each other, just standing in a tight closed circle, unable to stop laughing, laughing until the tears ran down our cheeks.

The weather turned bright and clear that last week in August.

We took my father's boat out every day, sailing to Violet's island, listening to QXR or ABC, the three of us happily lounging on deck and soaking up sunshine, going in for a swim whenever we felt like it. We saw Rhoda again maybe once or twice before the summer ended, but then only casually at Mr. Porter's or down on the dock, playing with the younger kids near the pilings. We always said hello to her, and she always answered shyly, her eyes turned away, "Hello," her metal bands catching sunlight for just an instant before she ducked her head.

The Greensward season ended officially on Labor Day, but most of the summer people left the island on the Saturday or Sunday before. In fact, they had to run four additional ferries that Sunday to accommodate the heavy traffic. Our families caught the nine o'clock boat out, trotting down to the dock with the rest of the islanders, all of us looking like gypsies, carrying belongings wrapped in blankets, bulging suitcases, bird cages, bicycles—it was a regular exodus scene. The two fags, Stuart and Frankie, came running onto the dock at the very last minute, carrying Violet's valises. Out of breath, wearing pendant earrings and white makeup, smelling of pumpkin, she allowed Stuart to help her aboard, and then stood on deck with both of them and waved tearfully at the island as the ferry horn sounded twice in warning.

A sharp wind was rising off the bay.

The ferry eased away from the dock, there was the clanging of bells, the engines were reversed, the boat slipped out into the water, away from the island. Violet stood on the port bow with her arms around her boys, whispering.

On the starboard bow, David, Sandy, and I huddled together against the wind.

We talked softly as the boat moved further and further away from the island. The wind was very sharp by the time we reached the center of the bay. Sandy put her arms around us, and we grinned and embraced her, but the wind was very cutting, it sliced through our clothes, it raged across the deck and finally drove Violet and the two boys inside to sit with the others.

We stayed on deck, huddled together.

It almost seemed as if winter had already come.

## Bestsellers from SIGNET

☐ **BLUE MOVIE by Terry Southern.** The author of RED-DIRT MARIJUANA and **Candy** has outdone himself with this bawdy, bizarre and bitingly satiric look at the making of "blue-movies." The cast of characters are a staggering variety of sexual deviants who help to make BLUE MOVIE the "bluest" book ever. "Murderously funny."—**Los Angeles Times** (#Y4608—$1.25)

☐ **BOMBER by Len Deighton.** With documentary precision and great story-telling skill, Len Deighton, the author of **The Ipcress File,** has created a powerful, panoramic account of a bombing raid during World War II. Declared a masterpiece by British critics, BOMBER is the most acclaimed and popular novel of postwar Great Britain. "The final impact of Bomber stuns . . ."—**The Washington Post** (#W4814—$1.50)

☐ **THE SUMMIT by Stephen Marlowe.** Intrigue, blackmail, treachery and romance, THE SUMMIT is a wire-taut novel as devious as LeCarré, as fast moving as Ambler or Greene—chosen by **The New York Times Book Review** as one of The Year's Best Criminals at Large, 1970 . . . "A shining example of the political extrapolation that pumped new lifeblood into the espionage novel in 1970." (#Y4632—$1.25)

☐ **SANCTUARY V by Budd Schulberg.** A gripping study of men and women under the most extreme kinds of pressure in a Cuban political haven. Writing with power, compassion, and with a rare gift for characterization, Budd Schulberg reconfirms with SANCTUARY V his position as one of America's master storytellers. (#Y4511—$1.25)

---

**THE NEW AMERICAN LIBRARY, INC.,**
P.O. Box 999, Bergenfield, New Jersey 07621

Please send me the SIGNET BOOKS I have checked above. I am enclosing $_____(check or money order—no currency or C.O.D.'s). Please include the list price plus 15¢ a copy to cover mailing costs.

Name_____

Address_____

City_____State_____Zip Code_____
Allow at least 3 weeks for delivery

◯

## Other SIGNET Titles You Will Want to Read